Lewis Clinton Strang

Players and Plays

Of the last quarter century. Vol. 2 (The Theatre of To-Day)

Players and Plays

Lewis Clinton Strang

Players and Plays
Of the last quarter century. Vol. 2 (The Theatre of To-Day)

ISBN/EAN: 9783337396725

Printed in Europe, USA, Canada, Australia, Japan

Cover: Foto ©Andreas Hilbeck / pixelio.de

More available books at **www.hansebooks.com**

Players and Plays
of the
Last Quarter Century

An Historical Summary of Causes and a Critical
Review of Conditions as Existing in the American
Theatre at the Close of the Nineteenth Century

By Lewis C. Strang

Volume II.

THE THEATRE OF TO-DAY

Illustrated

Boston

L. C. Page & Company

MDCCCCIII

CONTENTS

LIST OF ILLUSTRATIONS

List of Illustrations

PLAYERS AND PLAYS OF THE LAST QUARTER CENTURY

VOLUME II.

THE THEATRE OF TO-DAY

CHAPTER I.

ROBERTSON AND THE ENGLISH DRAMA

IN a little book called "The Dramatic Unities," which was published in 1874, Edwin Simpson wrote: "On reading over these old plays (the dramas of the Restoration), it is melancholy to see what a noble heritage has been bequeathed to us, and how sadly we have disgraced it. For two hundred years the English stage was as much above the French as the French, in the present day, is above our own. But, it is said, the French stage owes its excellence to the extreme liberty accorded to its writers in their choice of subjects. By no means. The French stage is great in spite of its immorality, and not on account of it. Look at the extraordinary skill in construction displayed by their writers; look at the freshness of their plots, and the originality of incidents which tend to their development; look at the wonderful little surprises, which, like an ' avoidance ' in music, excite the interest of the spectators in the highest degree, only agreeably to disappoint them. All these are excellences quite independent of the violation of social laws or the sanctity of the marriage tie. . . . Take them as specimens of constructive art, or as pictures of manners, and then say what have we to show against them. But patience! Already there are signs of better things. In those rare cases, within the last few years, where pieces written with some slight regard for nature and for common sense have been produced, they have been eagerly welcomed. There is no reason to doubt, then, that the public will again, whenever it may get the opportunity, prefer such pieces to the wild nonsense which is usually set before it."

At the present time it can be rightfully claimed that the English theatre has a drama of its own, and that Mr. Simpson's modest prophecy has been to an appreciable extent fulfilled. Whether the modern English drama is equal to the modern French or the modern German drama, is another proposition, and one that would carry the argument into lines too digressing at present to follow. The assertion may be made, however, that, while there is a finer appreciation of technique and a nicer sense of construction evidenced by the average French dramatist, it is an open question whether the general run of modern French drama outranks perceptibly the general run of modern English drama. There is more high class French drama, and it is treated more seriously as a literary product; it is criticised, theorised over, and fostered more intelligently and to better purpose; but even with all that, its quality, underneath the highly finished veneering, is by no means startling.

As between the German and the English drama, the difference is due more to national temperament than it is to diverse views as regards the function of the stage. The average

German citizen is a more serious animal than the average English citizen. The German turns more readily and more naturally to the contemplation of the speculative and the philosophical. He does not actually accomplish any more — not so much, probably — as his English brother, but he ponders better; and, therefore, he is more susceptible to the efforts of the dramatist with a theory to expound or a problem to analyse. This quality in the German temperament has brought into existence a drama, peculiar to the Fatherland, that, superficially at least, seems seriously worth while. It is to be questioned whether it really is, however; whether, after all, it achieves even momentarily the pearl of great price, which is truth; whether it does anything more than to stir up, until it smells to heaven more foully than before, the sociological mire, which every one knows is there, and above which one must rise before he can comprehend the good, the true, and the beautiful.

In one definite particular, however, both France and Germany have a decided advantage over England and America — that is in their subsidised theatres, which continue along the even tenor of their way regardless both of public taste and public patronage. Not only do they maintain a standard in acting, but they accomplish the far more valuable service of keeping alive as acted plays the scholarly and the classic drama of the nation. They are the public libraries of the drama, in which are preserved the literary treasures of the masters; they are the universities of the drama, the educators and the refiners of public taste, and as such they wield a vast influence for the ideal as against the merely mercenary and the instantaneously popular. Bereft of anything that even remotely resembles a national theatre, the wonder is, not that theatrical taste in Great Britain and the United States is not as high as it might be, but rather that theatrical taste, constantly at the mercy of the willy-nilly standard of box-office receipts, and generally measured by its cash value to a speculative manager of little or no artistic ambitions, is not lower than it actually is. The fact that any drama in the least worthy has been developed amid such adverse conditions speaks well for the predominate " tone " of the English-speaking people.

With possibly a reservation in favour of
Richard Lalor Sheil's "Evadne" and "The
Apostate," and James Sheridan Knowles's
"Virginius," the English stage from 1805 to
1830 was absolutely barren of any original
drama. Even in the instances of the plays
mentioned, their vogue was due more to the
popularity or the strength of certain actors,
than it was to any especial quality in the
works themselves. Thus the fascinations of
Eliza O'Neill were mainly responsible for the
reputation of "Evadne," while the genius of
Junius Brutus Booth was the leading factor
in keeping alive interest in "The Apostate."
Macready gave "Virginius" its first impetus,
and Forrest, and later John McCullough, did
their part toward promoting its longevity.
Had not the French drama burst forth into
such a glorious bloom in the years following
1830, when Victor Hugo's "Hernani" finally
dissipated the shadow of two centuries of
French classicism, it is likely that dramatic
writers, encouraged by a popular demand for
new plays, would have turned from the novel
and the newspaper to woo fame and fortune
on the English stage. Unfortunately for the

English drama, however, this demand for original work was met and satisfied for the time
by immense borrowings from foreign dramatic
sources.   Such a manufacturer of plays as
Dion Boucicault, for instance, "the adaptive
Mr. Boucicault," as Percy Fitzgerald termed
him, might have accomplished something far
beyond "London Assurance," "Old Heads and
Young Hearts," and "The Colleen Bawn,"
had he been obliged to develop his own original resources instead of being able to pounce
upon most of his material ready made.   Working mechanically and without thought, Boucicault never became anything more than an
actor's dramatist, who knew the stage and
whose animal spirits were unflagging.   Boucicault never laboured with an original motive
nor ever drew a genuinely human character.
He pleased the audiences of his day, and he
provided ways and means beloved by actors.
In this last circumstance reposes the real reason why Boucicault's plays are occasionally
given even now.   There is an actor demand for
them, and this is mistaken for a public demand.

Practically the same conditions hold regarding Sir Edward Bulwer-Lytton's "immortal"

dramas, " The Lady of Lyons " and " Richelieu," and Sheridan Knowles's " classics," " The Hunchback " and " The Love Chase." A long line of actors, including Booth, the crowning Richelieu of them all, kept that play alive by the force and the picturesqueness of their embodiment of the title part. It is, indeed, the best of Bulwer-Lytton's dramatic works, and in spite of — perhaps because of — its weighty verbosity, it remains to-day a fine type of melodrama. Its paramount merit is its delineation of the character of Richelieu, a part that in its theatrical phases is thrilling, picturesque, and emotionally striking. For that reason, the play has long been a favourite with both actors and spectators. Its chief structural blemish is the offensive theatricalism, which, after the catastrophe has been finally accomplished with the aid of a purely mechanical device, perpetrates the absurdity of making the leading character a dead man one minute and a very live one the next. No actor ever raised the last scene of " Richelieu " a single notch above cheap sensationalism.

There is some excuse for " Richelieu," but to find any defence for " The Lady of Lyons," judging the work by any conceivable standard of art, is wholly impossible. Yet it was a successful play in its day; and because there is still a theatrical thrill in it, and because it has "stunts" that the actor likes to perform, it has lived a fairly regular life ever since. However, it is doubtful if it can escape much longer that oblivion to which many far better plays than "The Lady of Lyons" were long ago consigned. To learn the reason why it has lasted as long as it has, one must strip the drama of its fine writing, its ponderous talk, its lines under the weight of which the bloodiest tragedy ever written would helplessly stagger. Behind all this rubbish will be found the framework of a first-class melodrama of the sentimental order, — a melodrama, the theme of which (the rough-running love of a lad, "born of poor, but honest parents," for a girl above his station, haughty and proud, — though of fond heart and trusting nature) has, since the world began, been a power with the romantically minded; and we are all of us romantically minded, when romance is so presented that it appeals to the especial weakness of our individual natures. Because it was during its youth effective with audiences whose sophistry was still quiescent, "The Lady of Lyons" acquired its unmerited reputation as a "literary" drama.

During the spring of 1902 "The Lady of Lyons" was utilised for a short tour of the United States.   The play was bravely arrayed in the finest of trappings, and twin stars — Miss Mary Mannering and Mr. Kyrle Bellew — shed upon it the effulgence of their glory.   Seeing it acted, however, was a curiously archaic experience, which proved one fact most conclusively, — to wit, that, regardless of how excellent they may be in the drama of their day, modern actors are hopelessly at sea when it comes to translating the high-flying Bulwer-Lytton language into anything at all resembling flesh and blood reality.   The modern actor simply does not know what to do with the excess of words that Bulwer-Lytton lavished on his play.   The lines frighten him ; he tries to make them sound "natural;" he tries to talk as he would talk if he met a friend on the street.   As a result he is continually embarrassed by the incongruity of his position, and he establishes no sort of an illusion.

MARY MANNERING

As Pauline in "The Lady of Lyons"

A play like " The Lady of Lyons " no more approximates reality than does a comic opera, and therefore it cannot be acted as if it had some relation to reality. To act it realistically immediately brings into the foreground precisely the faults that must at any cost be glossed over ; it means the deliberate uncovering of all the falsity, all the stiltedness, and all the sentimentality. To shy at Bulwer-Lytton's buncombe simply makes all the plainer the fact that there is something to shy at. Bold effrontery is the actor's only salvation. He must sail right in. He must tackle the heroics as if he were thoroughly convinced that he was a hero. He must plunge straight into the sentimentality with never a regard for sincerity and truth, and he must swallow the mush without stopping to taste it or to ascertain its flavour. The " grand style " is a poor style for an R. C. Carton comedy, but it is the only style that will make a Bulwer-Lytton melodrama endurable.

In the 1902 production of the play Kyrle Bellew, who acted Claude Melnotte, caught this manner finely in the garden scene with Pauline in the second act, and also in the scene in the following act, depicting the disillusion-

ising of Pauline after the marriage.   Miss Mary
Mannering was entirely unfitted by training to
show anything more than seductive sweetness
in her presentation of Pauline.   Mrs. W. G.
Jones, as the Widow Melnotte, displayed the
" grand manner " to the best advantage of all.
This veteran actress of years of experience in
the stock company of the Old Bowery Theatre,
thoroughly knew her business when it came to
acting a part in " The Lady of Lyons."   She
had breadth and freedom and authority; she
gave everything its full melodramatic value.
Still she did not overact, but kept always well
within both the part and the picture.   She
never shuddered, not even at the famous line,
" No divorce can separate a mother from her
son," but let it sweep out over the footlights as if
she believed that it meant something; and her
reward for so doing was a solid round of applause.

Sheridan Knowles's " The Hunchback " was
also acted in the United States in the spring
of 1902, with Viola Allen as Julia, Eben Plympton as Master Walter, Jameson Lee Finney as
Modus, Aubrey Boucicault as Sir Thomas Clif-
ford, C. Leslie Allen as Fathom, and Adelaide

VIOLA ALLEN
As Julia in "The Hunchback"

Prince as Helen. The seventy-year-old comedy, cut and slashed though it was in the process of reduction within the two hour and a half limit, endured the process of revival in excellent fashion, for its presentation by Miss Allen and her companions was good enough to emphasise its merits and minimise its defects. For this satisfactory result one did not go far astray in thanking Mr. Plympton, who staged the play and also acted Master Walter with comforting authority and delightful finish. There was homogeneity in the performance and unity in the acting, both of which manifested the guiding hand of one thoroughly familiar with the material dealt with.

The modern style of abbreviated dramatic writing was not in vogue when " The Hunchback " first made its appearance on the stage. Then it was quite the correct thing for characters to talk a great deal. A playwright was in duty bound to furnish at least a line for every emotion, and he would have considered himself disgraced and unworthy of his profession if he had permitted a character to feel any sort of a thrill without telling every one within hearing all about it. Of course, playwrights knew that men and women did not talk as their stage personages talked; in fact, the playwrights themselves compiled the paroxysms of language only at the expense of much brain-sweating. On the other hand, no dramatist in the thirties had any bothersome notions about it being the function of the drama to reproduce life; and, moreover, there was in those days no public content to gaze into a mirror that reflected nothing but nature. At that time fine writing was a part of the theatre, and the artificiality of fine writing was not perceived, much less resented. There was also in those days a race of actors who, breathing this atmosphere of artificiality all their professional lives, became so imbued with it that it was to them simply a manifestation of the art which approximates nature. Finding, in the many-worded sentences, what, to this perverted sense, seemed to be reality, they were able to speak those sentences with sincerity. Through constant practice with long recitations, they learned to utilise to the best advantage, in the conveying of emotion, in the forcing of illusion, and in the unmasking of the finest shades of meaning, the magic power of the speaking voice, that most beautiful and intricate of all instruments. They were not "natural," these players, but in their own drama, their artificiality secured an effect that to the spectator seemed natural, for the players were in harmony with their medium.

It was this emphatic theatrical style that Mr. Plympton succeeded most admirably in introducing into the company that supported Miss Allen, and it was this style that he himself affected in his acting of Master Walter. Picking his impersonation to pieces, one saw readily enough that it was composed of the most flamboyant theatricalism,—of emphatically pointed gestures, of accentuated facial expression, of starts and pauses and significant glances, all done with the utmost deliberation and with a definite purpose. This was not nature, and Mr. Plympton did not intend that it should be; but it was appropriate art to give Knowles's comedy the nearest possible relationship to nature. Even as the part was acted, so were the lines read,—not naturally, but with the precise elocution that suited them. Treated thus, their stiltedness faded away, and they became Master Walter's characteristic expression.

By this excellent performance, it was made plain that " The Hunchback " had not lived seventy years without possessing some very positive virtues. It may be written in old-fashioned style; its complicated story, revealing countless absurdities joined together by means of the weakest assumptions, may be declared impossible, rather than merely improbable. Yet there must be something compelling about the tale to keep it still in existence. I think that it is the strong romantic flavour in both " The Hunchback " and " The Lady of Lyons " that makes their appeal so potent. They do, in their unidealistic way, deal directly with idealism; they picture an imaginative world utterly removed from the prosaic, and people it with personages who sip continually nectar and who eat nought but ambrosia. The world is hungry for the ideal, though it is generally blind to what the ideal actually is. The imagination, playing with the material things with which it is most familiar, pictures heaven in many strange disguises. One of these disguises is the never-was world of romance, with its sentimental love, its priggish and effeminate men, and its flat and insipid women. In this world "The Hunchback" has its place, and there successive generations of theatre-goers seek it with praise and thanksgiving.

In this summing up of the strong points of "The Hunchback," let there not be ignored the influence of the subplot, in which Modus and Helen are particularly concerned. Always a living representation of the way of a maid with a man, the comedy therein enshrined is still fresh and vigorous, for does it not declare plainly the insinuating charm of the original Eve?

Robert Browning's "Strafford" and "The Blot in the 'Scutcheon," the latter a strongly fateful tragedy, emotionally impressive and poetically alluring, failed to secure the popular esteem that was accorded Doctor Westland Marston's very formal tragedies, which passed from life and remembrance long ago. Even as Dion Boucicault was fortunate in his entrance into the school of artificial comedy with his "London Assurance," securing for that work unmerited rank with the standard comedies, so Tom Taylor and Charles Reade, largely through the acting possibilities enfolded in

Peg Woffington, were fortunate with " Masks and Faces." Taylor also produced " Still Waters Run Deep " and " The Ticket-of-Leave Man," plays of more than average art, though, with " Masks and Faces," of probable foreign origin. Besides these, Talfourd's tragedy in verse, " Ion," should be recalled.

Such is the meagre array of original drama for the thirty odd years after 1830 — drama, that is to say, with sufficient positive merit to remain on the stage long enough to be remembered. Countless other plays there were, but they are largely only names, which one finds in theatrical histories or in the biographies of the great actors. Of course, popularity is a poor test of artistic merit. Yet it is a question if there is any really great art that does not awaken a responsive echo in even the least cultured of human beings. The vital fact in art is truth, and truth is real, absolute, and universal in its appeal. Therefore, while the drama which does not reflect truth may secure an instant's vogue, its doom is, nevertheless, sealed and certain. While the drama that does reflect truth may not at the moment attract wide-spread attention, its immortality, even though that immortality be expressed as an influence or as an effect on individuals, is assured. The constant characteristic of all this middle-of-the-century English drama was its lack of truth, its lifelessness. It treated of a world that never existed, in a manner that never was; it represented men and women that were not, governed by motives and impelled by sentiments that were fictitional and ridiculous. It lacked the compelling and vitalising quality of universal humanity, which, in the face of all subservient faults and shortcomings, gives power and direction to every variety of artistic production.

Keeping well before one the essential dryness and lifelessness of this drama, it is possible to understand how it happened that a playwright, whose work was intrinsically of no great worth, came to figure in a mild way as the saviour of the English theatre, as the founder of a new school of play-writing, and as the inspirer of a new drama. In some such relation to the English drama of to-day stands Tom W. Robertson, whose period of productive activity was only between 1865 and 1870. His comedies were acted as follows: " Society," in November, 1865; "Ours," in September, 1866; "Caste," in April, 1867; "Play," in February, 1868; "School," in January, 1869; and "M. P.," in April, 1870. There is no defence possible, nor is any demanded, for Robertson's faults; his plays are flimsy, inconsequential, sentimental, sloppy, and inane. Nevertheless, it is a fact that for twenty or more years Robertson was the ruling influence in English comedy. Moreover, it was he that gave to English comedy the thrust forward that severed it to a degree from the fanciful existence conjured by half a century of theatrical imaginings; it was he that turned it again in the direction of truth. The mild impetus imparted by Robertson, gathering force and authority in its plunge down the last years of the century, made possible the English comedy of to-day, by far the best comedy since Goldsmith and Sheridan, and comedy, moreover, that ranks well with similar achievements in the foreign theatres. It is quite worth while, therefore, to avoid any unnecessary discussion of Robertson's all too obvious faults, and try instead to ascertain what were the merits that made his effect on the theatre of his time and of his immediate succeeding so great and so permanent.

William Archer thus neatly contrasted Robertson and Tom Taylor: " If Mr. Robertson had had some of Mr. Tom Taylor's culture, taste, and constructive talent, or Mr. Taylor some of Mr. Robertson's fresh humour and mastery of the minutiæ of stage business, we should have had one admirable instead of two imperfect playwrights. Mr. Taylor's mind was exclusively prosaic. There was nothing of the *genial* about him, — I use the word in its German sense, — while T. W. Robertson was undeniably *genial*, with all his shortcomings."

Robertson was not a man of unusual mental capacity. He was neither a student nor a philosopher. Life in the abstract did not in the least interest him. His ethical perception was meagre, and questions of right and wrong, moral problems, or sociological conditions, suggested nought of the dramatic to him. The superficialities of society and the commonplace social relations he utilised as dramatic themes. He viewed all these things from the outside. He did not probe for causes, but was wholly content to picture conditions as he saw them, for the specific and definite purpose of entertaining the multitude. As he treated society, so Robertson treated men and women. Reduced to their lowest terms, his characters are colourless figures on which are hung certain mannerisms and peculiarities. They are veritable shadows dressed up in sure-enough clothes, so that they look like men and women. When filled out and vivified by the actor's personality, they become sufficiently substantial to pass muster under ordinary inspection as men and women. Combined with a naïveness that was a genuine novelty in the theatre, with a spontaneity that was invigorating, and with a humour that was thoroughly alive, Robertson's externals quite naturally captivated and subdued that public to which they were first offered, a public that had not had its stomach turned by an overabundance of such cloy sweetness and insipid sentimentality.

Purely as acted drama and solely as an appeal to unsophisticated spectators, Robertson's plays seemed — and would seem to this day, if they could be acted before the same unsophisticated audiences — positively delightful. His smack of realism gave verisimilitude to his situations and his characters, making them both charmingly familiar. His sentiment, however false to the analytical sense, seemed sweet and delicate and pretty; it suggested pathos, and it gave a touch of idealism to the ordinary. His wit was neither so wide as a river nor so deep as a well, but it sufficed: the point was not so sharp that it pricked before it was perceived. His humour, which was the single genuine thing about Robertson, sprinkled gently the whole fabric of his work, causing the wrinkles to vanish and the meagreness to expand into an illusionary imitation of substance. In short, Robertson's triumph was the triumph of the ordinary and the conventional, a triumph that is as old as the history of literature. There was the seeming evidence of truth in Robertson's comedies. His externals were sufficiently redolent with it to be momentarily deceptive. Familiarity with Robertson, however, could not fail to breed contempt. Holes appeared in the cloth of his drama, and fleshless bones poked into sight. Lacking substance, devoid of any positive grip on the reality of things, and giving expression to no enduring quality of beauty,

Robertson's plays soon ceased to exist as entities. Such accents of truth as they did voice were not lost, but passed into the consciousness of the people. They became, in fact, a strong influence in the English theatre, an influence that made possible dramatic achievements as much farther removed from Robertson as Robertson himself was removed from the drama that immediately preceded him.

It is an interesting comparison, — that between Tom Robertson and W. S. Gilbert, Robertson's direct successor in the field of English comedy. Both were protests against artificiality, bombast, and emotional formalism. Yet, except in the single particular that both were innocently obvious in their dramatic methods, their character delineation, and their plot development, they were entirely different in their mental equipment. Robertson was painstakingly conventional, while Gilbert was painstakingly unconventional. Gilbert was fully as much a pamphleteer and a critic as he was a dramatist, and it was temperamentally impossible for him to avoid making a point, never mind how much he violated character or

MARY ANDERSON

As Galatea in " Pygmalion and Galatea."

situation in so doing. In his pursuit of the vastly different, he was continually going to extremes. Thus " The Palace of Truth," with its startling reversals of the ordinary, was too logically illogical to be grasped by the impressionable, but rarely thoughtful theatre audience. In his peculiarly Gilbertian way, Gilbert worked with the same platitudes that Robertson did : but while Robertson strove to make these platitudes seem novel by breathing into them a trifle of freshness and originality, Gilbert ruthlessly uncovered their pretensions, and, by turning them upside down, revealed relentlessly their absurdities. Gilbert's two best dramatic works were " Pygmalion and Galatea " and " Comedy and Tragedy." The first is still a great favourite with actresses ; and although it is written around the trite theme of a statue coming to life, its conceits are so daintily handled, there is such a wealth of wit in its lines, and its digs at human foibles and frailties are so pointed, that even to this day its consistent impression is that of fascinating novelty and originality. " Comedy and Tragedy " was written especially for Mary Anderson, who was well received in it. There are, however, acting possibilities in the play which no actress has as yet completely realised.

W. S. Gilbert was thoroughly individual from the beginning to the end of his career, so individual, in fact, that no one has ever been able in any degree to reproduce his particular quality of wit, satire, and burlesque.

When one man takes a step forward in any line of the world's work, there always appear about him many men, who are striving valiantly to follow in his footsteps and to reap the benefits of his enterprise. Robertson's popular success was remarkable, and naturally there assembled a mighty herd of imitators, anxious to occupy the fertile fields that he had cultivated. It is usually the way under such conditions that the faults of the original are pretty thoroughly threshed out before the influence of his virtues begins to be felt. It was so with Robertson, and the playwrights that immediately succeeded him, nearly all of them writing in a vein distinctly reminiscent of Robertson, were without exception even more inconsequential, sloppy, and flimsy than the dramatist from whom they derived their inspiration; and, in addition, they introduced into their work an inherent insincerity from which Robertson was largely free.

Of the lot, the most widely popular and the most representative was Henry J. Byron, best known through the success of his play, " Our Boys," which at one time seemed likely to run for ever. He was a prolific writer, but he was entirely without solidity. His plays had neither plots nor characters, though he was a consistent punster and a notable antic in his use of English. Byron's contemporary, James Albery, wrote excellent dialogue, but he lacked constructive talent, taste, and earnestness. There were charming bits in most of his plays, among them " Apple Blossoms " and " Forgiven," instances both of fanciful wit and of witty fancy; but they were spoiled by their indefiniteness and incoherency, and the touch of caricature that was fixed on nearly all of their characters. George R. Sims, the typical Cockney, also gained considerable recognition as a dramatist, although he was a much better journalist than he was play-maker. " The Member of Slocum," done by Nat C. Goodwin early in his starring career, was well liked in the United States, and " The Lights o' London," a melodrama with many excellent touches in the depicting of low life in the English metropolis, was also a success on this side of the water. It perfectly illustrated Sims's instinct for the theatrically effective both as regards pathos and humour. He was strictly, possibly purposely, conventional, and he always remembered that the small boy in the gallery was an important factor in the financial success of a play. Into this same class came the Arthur Wing Pinero and the Henry Arthur Jones of youthful experience, but the latter works of these two modern dramatists entitled them to higher rank. By those, therefore, it is only just to judge them.

The writers of serious plays in the seventies and early eighties were not many. Alfred Tennyson had the desire to be a dramatist, and " The Cup " was fairly well received in the theatre. Tennyson, however, never fairly sized up the stage, and his writings for the theatre, while often imaginative and ennobling in conception, were never vitally dramatic. Herman Charles Merivale produced something rather better than the ordinary melodrama in " Forget-Me-Not," in which, as

Stephanie, both Genevieve Ward and Rose Coghlan were unusually successful. It was a play of intrigue, developed with strong theatrical effect. The opposition between Stephanie, the adventuress who had fastened her foul presence on a helpless young woman, and the lover of this young woman, the man of the world, keen of intellect and thoroughly skilled in artifice, provided a motive pregnant with dramatic interest of a melodramatic order. The tension was capitally maintained throughout, and the solution was ingenious, unforced, and of itself theatrically effective. The play also dealt by suggestion with a very positive social problem, and this fact alone gave it some additional noteworthiness, inasmuch as at the time that the drama appeared, the English theatre was especially lacking in thoughtfulness.

W. G. Wills, whose " The Man o' Airlie " gave Lawrence Barrett, as James Harebell, a chance to do his most effective work in a pathetic line, was by no means a strong or a sure dramatic writer; but he was fortunate in early falling under the tender nursing of Henry Irving, whose influential productions gave to the work of Mr. Wills a certain amount of dignity, and placed it directly in line for serious criticism. Thoroughly representative, — indeed, probably the best of Mr. Wills's plays, — was "Charles I.," which Mr. Irving found good enough to retain in his repertory. It was a curious play, evidently written with the purpose of vindicating Charles I. and vilifying Cromwell. Whether one agreed or disagreed with Mr. Wills's treatment of the unfortunate Charles Stuart might have depended largely on the history one had read, but it is doubtful if in any history Mr. Wills found warrant for his slander of Oliver Cromwell. Historical accuracy, of course, has nothing whatsoever to do with play-writing, and probably no one would have concerned himself greatly regarding Mr. Wills's private opinion of Charles and Cromwell, if the dramatist had not so insistently thrust it into the foreground. It was not so much in fact, but in character that Mr. Wills departed from what is generally accepted as the truth about Charles I. Ignoring completely the fact that Cromwell and his commoners had the right on their side, however harsh and unreasonable they may have been

MISS ELLEN TERRY
As Henrietta Maria in " Charles I."

in enforcing their rights, Mr. Wills idealised Charles to the utmost, and emphasised the martyr idea in every possible way. He did these things adroitly by keeping constantly in view the human side rather than the kingly side of Charles. One saw Charles in the home circle, playing with his children and comforting his wife even while he himself was perplexed and harassed by his enemies. One heard the high-sounding sentiment of Charles's loyal friends, the loving tribute of his queen, the tender prattlings of the little prince and princess. There was never a hint of the despot. Charles was consistently portrayed as a fearfully abused monarch, while the harsh-spoken Oliver Cromwell became a melodramatic villain and a despicable beggar for bribes.

There is no quarrel with Mr. Wills for picturing Charles as a martyr. In so doing he but paralleled the opinion of all stalwart Jacobites. Mr. Wills's fault was in overdoing the thing, and thereby lapsing into obvious sentimentality. He made Charles so very good, so exceedingly meek, and so tremendously long-suffering, that he well-nigh took all the royalty out of him and came near establishing him as a slightly ridiculous figure. A king — even a bad king — put to death by his subjects is of itself a tragedy. The event brings a striking contrast before the imagination, and it is, therefore, dramatically valuable. But the last sad farewells of a spiritless man, who has met fate with hands self-consciously folded and eyes affectedly uplifted, is sentimentally lovely, perhaps, and may be even momentarily pathetic; but it is not the sort of spectacle, nor is such a king the sort of man, deeply to stir the emotions.

CHAPTER II.

AT the head of English dramatic writers of the present time is Arthur Wing Pinero, whose right to this preëminence has not been challenged since the production in 1893 of "The Second Mrs. Tanqueray," which, immediately preceded by that most enjoyable light comedy, "The Amazons," made manifest both Mr. Pinero's artistic seriousness and his versatility. Pinero's career has been strikingly successful, and one of steady growth as well. His failures have been surprisingly few, though that fact alone would be of no value whatever in proving his standing as a dramatist. Nor, on the other hand, should Mr. Pinero be thought any the less of, because he has shown a remarkable instinct in sizing up his public. Success is not a crime, except, possibly, in the eyes of the person that always fails; and, in fact, while the great and indefinite public may find enjoyment in many plays that are hopelessly devoid of art, and may also condemn plays of honest artistic worth, it is equally true that there must be some positive art in that which habitually brings a response from the great and indefinite public. Hence, other things being equal, Mr. Pinero is entitled to all the more credit on account of his success.

Mr. Pinero, moreover, has never written down to the public, and he has always been consistent in his endeavour to please first of all himself. He has never yielded to the temptation that so generally assails the successful playwright, — the temptation to increase the quantity of his output at the expense of the quality. In his younger days, Mr. Pinero was an exceedingly rapid workman. Thus his second production, the comedietta, "Two Hundred a Year," was written in a single afternoon. "Lords and Commons" was finished in ten days, and "Dandy Dick" in something over three weeks. For ten years past, however, Mr. Pinero has not averaged a play a year, and that, too, in the face of a demand for his work that can scarcely be overestimated.

There is artistic conscience behind this moderation, and artistic conscience is far more rare and far more desirable than avarice, which in the end is sure to injure vitally the one that cherishes it.

It is as a master of his craft, of the peculiar technique of the drama, that Mr. Pinero is most distinguished and most readily comprehended. Without a question, the stage is his exact and proper field of labour; and as a story teller, essayist, critic, or lecturer he is unknown. Mr. Pinero's appreciation of theatrical values and his mastery of the special conditions that hold in the theatre are absolute. Indeed, they amount to nothing short of genius. Victorien Sardou is usually called the master of stage-craft among contemporaneous playwrights; but Mr. Pinero in " The Gay Lord Quex " fairly eclipsed Sardou in his own specialty. Working for a single theatrical effect, Mr. Pinero so manipulated his characters, so arranged his preliminary situations, and to the end hid his machinery with such adroitness that, even when it was discovered, admiration for the dramatist's skill was quite strong enough to balance any disappointment over the essential artificiality of his scheme. One felt that he could like the play without shame, notwithstanding the deception of which he had been the victim. Sardou has rarely attained that height. His machinery is usually obvious, and his appeal gross and without subtilty. Though one may momentarily yield to it, he nevertheless recognises the falsity and the unworthiness of the emotion thus inspired; and he resents the playwright's power to move him, as an unwarranted violation of his individual rights.

Born in London in 1855, and beginning his active life as a student of law in his father's office, natural inclination early turned Pinero toward the theatre. In Edinburgh, in June, 1874, he made his début as an actor, and he remained an actor until 1882, the last six years of that period being passed as a member of Henry Irving's company at the Lyceum Theatre, London. Pinero's playwriting began in 1877, when the comedietta, " Two Can Play at That Game," was produced at the Lyceum. " Two Hundred a Year " followed in short order. " Daisy's Escape " was brought out in 1879, and " Hester's Mystery," " Bygones," and " The Money Spinner " came

in 1880. The last mentioned directed attention to the dramatist and did much permanently to establish him. "Imprudence" and
"The Squire," which Thomas Hardy tried in
vain to prove was borrowed from his novel,
"Far from the Madding Crowd," were acted
in 1881; "Lords and Commons" and "The
Rocket" in 1883; "The Ironmaster," adapted
from Ohnet's "Le Maître des Forges," and
"Low Water" in 1884. The series of court
farces was started in 1885, and they were
"The Magistrate" (1885), "The Schoolmis-
tress" and "The Hobby Horse" in 1886, and
"Dandy Dick" (1887).

Beginning with "Sweet Lavender" in 1888,
a delicate comedy, somewhat sentimental in
tone, but touching a theme that was underlaid
with strength and even sombreness, Pinero
steadily grew in originality, individuality, and
authority. Up to that time, his average work,
while excelling in quality the efforts of Byron
and the other Robertsonian playwrights, was
distinctly of their class; Pinero was thoroughly imbued with the Robertsonian influence, though his product was, even then,
rather more virile than the plays on which it

was modelled. "Sweet Lavender" was followed the next year by "The Profligate," in which the sex problem, so fully exploited in "The Second Mrs. Tanqueray," was first touched upon. "The Weaker Sex," "The Cabinet Minister," "The Times," and "In Chancery," were also of this period. The last four were all farces, though in them could be traced the evidences of Pinero's increasing seriousness. For instance, in "The Cabinet Minister" there are the elements of a tragedy to offset the laughter, and the effect of the play is that of mingled mirth and pain. The story hovers about a pretty, though not brilliant woman, who marries into a social sphere with which she is not familiar. She pursues but never reaches her social Mecca, and, abandoning the chase after years of failure, tries to satisfy her discontent by lavish expenditures of money, which finally involve her family in ruin. Her unfitness for the position she holds as the wife of a cabinet minister is thus accentuated by the fact that she has made a bankrupt of her husband. Her first recourse is to the usurer, and next she yields to the temptations of dishonesty. Here, then, although it has its being in a farce, is an original study of character, a study that would appeal only to a man of imagination, and that could be vitalised dramatically only by a master.

"Lady Bountiful," a comedy of much quiet charm, which was produced in 1891, failed with the public, and nothing more was heard of Pinero until the spring of 1893, when "The Amazons" was acted. It was succeeded the same year by "The Second Mrs. Tanqueray." Although "The Amazons" was given to the public first, it was written after "The Second Mrs. Tanqueray," as a relief from the seriousness of that drama. Two more "problem plays," as this variety of drama was termed, were constructed before Pinero again turned to light comedy. Neither "The Notorious Mrs. Ebbsmith" nor "The Benefit of the Doubt," both given in 1895, had the directness or the honesty of "The Second Mrs. Tanqueray," and both were comparative failures. "The Princess and the Butterfly" was seen in 1897, "Trelawney of the Wells" in 1898, "The Gay Lord Quex" in 1899, and Pinero's last play, "Iris," in 1901.

In order best to get at Pinero's merits and demerits as a dramatist, it is necessary to examine somewhat in detail several of his representative plays, every one of which has substance enough to be able to stand such an examination. First on the list is, naturally enough, " The Second Mrs. Tanqueray; " and to avoid any misunderstanding, it will be well to rehearse the main points in the plot. Aubrey Tanqueray, a widower of some years' standing, whose first wife is vividly recalled by one of his friends as a creature of cold marble and black velvet, goes to the other extreme by choosing as his second mate a woman whose past has been more than a trifle torrid. Tanqueray expects social ostracism, and he gets it. Possibly, even at that, he might have worked out his problem, if his daughter by his first wife, a girl reared in the asceticism and narrowness of the convent, had not come home from school to live with him. The passionate longing of Paula Tanqueray for a love that is pure, sympathetic, compassionate, and ennobling fixes on Ellean as its object, but the girl's nature has not unfolded sufficiently to respond. Ellean permits the instinctive repugnance that she has for the woman who has sinned — albeit she does not herself know the precise cause for this repugnance — to rule her; and thus the single influence, a love forgiving and ideally charitable, that would have saved Paula, is denied her.

Up to this point, it is not too much to say that Pinero's play is a masterpiece. Right here he had the choice of two courses of action, — to depict Paula struggling to her redemption, aided and buoyed up by the strengthening power of Ellean's perfect love, or to depict Paula battling alone, desperately and futilely, against the overwhelming odds of accumulated errors. He chose the latter course, which was the more obvious and the less worthy, a course, moreover, that led him directly into a maze from which there was no escape except by the exercise of brute force.

Repulsed by Ellean and wounded to the core, resentful and jealous, Paula quarrels with her husband, quarrels with the only woman friend of her husband that was willing to do what she could to help the unfortunate couple, invites two friends from the old life to visit her, friends of whom she sickens as quickly as she sees them, and finally intercepts and delays letters to Tanqueray from Ellean and her chaperon, which, had they been read in time, might have averted the final catastrophe. For Ellean, on a visit to Paris, meets and loves and becomes betrothed to one of Paula's former lovers. The situation is a horrible one, from which one can figure no satisfactory escape, and probably Pinero's method of forcing the issue is as good as any other. Paula sends the young man away. Ellean guesses why, after a stormy interview with Paula, and then Paula herself commits suicide. Of course, this violence ends the play, though it is not in any sense a solution of the problem. The inevitable question therefore crops out, " What, after all, has it amounted to ? "

It should be understood that this question is not one of morals. There never was a more moral play written than " The Second Mrs. Tanqueray." Nor is it a question of the technique of play-writing. Pinero's construction is admirable in every way, a constant source of the keenest pleasure; and his faculty for securing on the stage the effect, practically perfect, of the social life of modern times leaves little

MRS. PATRICK CAMPBELL
As Paula Tanqueray in "The Second Mrs. Tanqueray"

or nothing to cavil over.   What could be more spontaneous or natural than the scene between the four men that opens the play?   And the men themselves — Tanqueray, nervous, uneasy, and wilfully blind to the foolishness of the marriage that he has resolved upon; the somewhat cynical Doctor Jayne and the worldly-wise Frank Misquith, bits, both of them, yet characters absolutely distinct, and that, too, without being in the least eccentric; finally the gossipy, good-hearted, honestly friendly, and thoroughly sensible Cayley Drummle.   Each character is so capably drawn as to be almost actor-proof, yet, in the hands of a skilled player, each is submissive to infinite expansion.

No, there is no quarrel with Pinero's morals or his technique; but his ethics and his judgment of what really constitutes a strong, intense, and inspiring drama do need correction. His vital mistake was made in the character of Ellean and in Ellean's relations to Paula. Had he given Ellean a heart and compassionate comprehension that would have felt Paula's unhappiness and understood how to bring out her inherent goodness, then Mr. Pinero would have provided himself with a golden opportunity for portraying regeneration instead of dissolution, for building up a noble character structure instead of dragging an unfortunate and protesting woman deeper and deeper into the Slough of Despond. I do not mean that Paula, if she had been sympathetically met by Ellean, would have become all at once an angel with sprouting wings. Such a course would have been far more absurd than the course that Mr. Pinero did adopt. Paula would of necessity have had her struggles. Indeed, she would have needed them in order to grow. She might possibly have failed in securing any material reward for her sincere effort to live down the past. Success or failure to-day or to-morrow, next year or within a lifetime, is of comparatively little importance, however, if only the struggle for what is good and true be consistent and enduring. Had Mr. Pinero chosen to portray such a struggle, even if he had felt it a necessity to overwhelm Paula with the multitude of her offences, he would have preached the optimism of reality instead of the pessimism of chaos and dissatisfaction.

" The Notorious Mrs. Ebbsmith " does not

begin to be as carefully and as adroitly written a play as " The Second Mrs. Tanqueray," and recognising that fact helps one to understand the success of the one and the comparative failure of the other. Give Pinero credit for one thing. Usually, when he starts to make a play, he has definitely in mind what he is going to do and what he is going to say. In " The Second Mrs. Tanqueray " he wanted to say a word for the woman, who, he believed, was not always fairly treated by society. In the case of " The Notorious Mrs. Ebbsmith," however, it would seem as if the flattering reception accorded " The Second Mrs. Tanqueray " has for the time deprived Mr. Pinero of his habitual keenness of perception and soundness of judgment. Without any especial or definite idea awaiting stage exposition, he sat himself down to try to do over again in a slightly different way precisely what he had already done in " The Second Mrs. Tanqueray; " and the result was " The Notorious Mrs. Ebbsmith," a play with a last act and three preceding ones.

The chief difficulty with these three first acts is that they do not contain a single active character to whom one can give his hearty coöperation except the Duke of St. Olpherts, and he has such a deservedly bad reputation that one dares only to whisper that he is at all likable.   But, whether he be moral or immoral, the duke has the advantage of knowing just where he stands; and in that particular he is such an improvement over Agnes and Cleeve that one almost unconsciously comes to regard him as a sort of haven of safety. The duke sees exactly the mistake that Agnes is making in living unlawfully with Cleeve, and in relying on any steadfastness of purpose in him, and he is sorry for her.   The duke remembers the deserted wife at home, and he is sorry for her.   He knows, too, what an egotist Cleeve is, and him he thoroughly despises.

Until Pinero reached the last act of the drama, and therein dragged Agnes by main force into the open and set her down face to face with the wife, — until, in fact, he made the visionist gaze upon herself with unhappy, disillusionised eyes, he had been striving merely for effect.   The taint of forced unreality had been constantly in evidence.   The dialogue, particularly that spoken by Agnes, had strained credulity and come dangerously near bombast. Even his theatrical Bible and stove episode did not make the impression that was expected from it, chiefly because Agnes's mental condition, which made her wish to burn the Bible, was not felt as a conviction. In the last act, however, Pinero had something to say and something to do. He had fully to reveal, so that even Agnes comprehended, the complete shallowness of Lucas Cleeve, to whose pitiful egotism, supreme selfishness, and inordinate vanity was due the misery that had so thickly clotted the play; and he had to show the self-sacrifice of which two women were capable for the man they loved, though they recognised fully that the man himself was wholly unworthy of that sacrifice. In the last act, therefore, Pinero got fairly on his feet and spoke for truth, thus in the final moments saving his work from utter condemnation.

" Trelawney of the Wells " is probably Pinero's best comedy of character. Passing by the Cavendish Square "swells," who, in contrast with the delightfully human actor-folk with which the play is peopled, seem exaggerated and unnatural, the drama is a remarkably homogeneous product; and, as is the case with every thoroughly dramatic work, it cannot be known for its full value until it has been seen on the stage. Unquestionably an important part of the charm of " Trelawney of the Wells " is due to the quaintness of the setting and the oddity of the costumes of the sixties. Pictorial effect in a drama may be ranked next as an essential to character and action. The danger is in emphasising pictorial effect at the expense of character and action, but this danger Pinero has adroitly avoided. As a portrayal of typical actor conditions, the comedy is truthful as well as interesting, though displaying no great depth of characterisation, and dealing more with types than with carefully defined men and women. It was evidently Pinero's purpose to reveal the personages in this play vividly and almost instantaneously; and save in the instance of Tom Wrench, the aspiring playwright, further logical development was not attempted. This touch-and-go quality gives to most of the characters the slightest element of delicate bur-

MARY MANNERING
As Rose in " Trelawney of the Wells "

lesque, which serves to bring out their humour without in the least detracting from their life-likeness.   Nor can one fail to be impressed by the love and the tenderness with which the dramatist has treated his players.   He has faithfully set forth their foibles, their weaknesses, and their vanities, but the hand that exposes these frailties is actuated by motives thoroughly sympathetic and kindly.   There is not a hint of bitterness nor of scorn.   The dramatist's interest in Tom Wrench is more deeply seated than is his interest in his actors, and there is inspired by the presentation of this character a sense of compassion, sweet, sincere, and beautiful.

Turning from " Trelawney of the Wells " to " The Gay Lord Quex " is like experiencing a sudden transition from the soft warmth of June to the keen, frosty, invigorating sparkle of wintry December.   " The Gay Lord Quex " is clean-cut, sharp, and intellectually exhilarating.   It is a decided mental stimulant, but there its effectiveness ends.   It never once touches the heart.   In short, the comedy is a masterpiece of dramatic construction and of theatrical effect, the practical perfection of artificiality; but it sets forth not a single personage in whom one finds a trace of vital interest. The play centres around a single situation, from which is forced the very limit of dramatic intensity. Preparing the way for this situation are two acts, which, while necessarily mechanical in their relations to the vital third act, are, nevertheless, so novel, picturesque, and ingenious that they hold the attention perfectly. Moreover, the last act, which is merely the perfunctory closing of the argument, contains so much of the same novelty and ingenuity that it, too, interests until the fall of the final curtain. The achievement was, indeed, a remarkable one, for the material with which the playwright laboured bordered on the insignificant. Sophy Fullgarney, the manicure girl, is a striking and an original conception, forcibly delineated by the dramatist, and, it may be added, forcibly realised by Miss Irene Vanbrough, the actress. The other characters, however, all of them individual and entertaining, cannot be termed in the least exciting. But it is the cleverness — to use a much abused word, which exactly fits "The Gay Lord Quex" — that is amazing; and the accumulative force of the action, which reaches its full sway in a third act of biting incisiveness, intense interest, perfect emotional contrast, splendidly utilised suspense, and unescapable climactic vigour, is a positive triumph of construction.

Analysis of this great third act will reveal the most perfect trickery in playing upon an audience's susceptibilities. Notice how softly it begins, with the Duchess of Strood and Mrs. Jack Eden in a before-bedtime gossip; how cautiously the little points are made; how innocently the details of architecture, the position of the halls and the doors, and especially the situation of Sophy's room, are explained. One gets them all, and then, if he stop to think, wonders how it happens that he knows so much. Notice how strongly the motive for Quex's attitude toward Sophy is insisted upon, — one is not merely led to suspect that she is listening at the door, nor is he left to the chance of hearing from her own lips that she has been listening; one has it strikingly demonstrated before his eyes that she is listening. Notice the constant pulling this way and that in the long scene between Quex and Sophy; the various steps by which Quex strengthens his position, until he has the woman reduced to an hysterical pulp; then thrill at the master-stroke by which the entire situation instantly changes and the woman is triumphant over the man; finally, admire the unforeseen but natural device by means of which the incident is closed. Now that it is all over, reflect by how much the action has been advanced or the characters developed during this breathless episode. Just to this extent, that Sophy has been made to believe that Quex may, perhaps, be a good enough husband for her Muriel.

"The Gay Lord Quex" is great as an example of masterful dramatic construction, but it is no more art than is the magnificent and highly complicated machinery which drives the ocean greyhound from Liverpool to New York in a few hours over five days.

It is plain from the examination of these four plays that Pinero is an adept in the mechanics of his profession, and that the drama is the one vehicle of expression which perfectly suits him; that his thought is broad, his imagination fertile, his versatility unusual, his humour and his wit essentially dramatic, finding their appeal and their point in the varying relations between character and action. His ability to present personages that live and create an environment that reflects life is also amply apparent.   What Pinero lacks — what, in fact, every modern playwright lacks — is deep-seated conviction and firmly grounded understanding of the fundamental facts of existence, of the realities and the ideals through the attaining of which mortals will solve the problem of their being.   Pinero and all of his confrères are superficial thinkers.   They observe the actions of men, and from these externals they try to deduce adequate motives and satisfactory reasons. They deal constantly in a detached way with detached bits from the panorama of worldly existence, and they have no determined principle by which the valuation of thoughts and deeds can be estimated, no standard by which thoughts and deeds can be measured, no fixed ideal in the light of which they can be studied, no key by means of which world mysteries can be unlocked.   Perplexed by the outward seeming, we find the dramatist declaring that there is no such thing as harmony, and reproducing in his dramas little else than perplexities and inconsistencies.   Thus he misses the primary art-essential, which is the realisation of the perfect unity of the good, the true, and the beautiful.

While the dramatist should be a deep student of men and of affairs, he should at the same time be a poet; that is to say, he should nourish as his most precious possession an abiding sense of spiritual reality. The modern dramatist, however, is just a little ashamed of spirituality, which he confounds with indefiniteness, impracticability, and utter foolishness. He does not consider deeply enough to perceive that the poet, beholding back of everything the spiritual first cause, has something positive on which to base a judgment; that it is the poet with a comprehension of what life really means, who is thereby able to harmonise inconsistencies and adequately to state motives; that it is the poet who is the seer and the prophet, whose instinct furnishes wisdom for the philosopher, and whose intuition enriches the theories of the problemists. Only a dramatist who is a poet and looks away from things material for his inspiration can become absolutely great, for only a poet can appreciate and can make others appreciate the ideality that is wedded to immortality.

HENRY ARTHUR JONES

Henry Arthur Jones, ranking next to Pinero among modern English dramatists, is four years Pinero's senior, though they both began writing for the theatre about the same time. Jones is what is sometimes called a "self-made" man. He was born on a farm in Buckinghamshire, and he started to earn his own living when he was thirteen years old. He never saw a dramatic performance until he was eighteen. Then at the London Haymarket he was thrilled with Kate Bateman's acting of Leah the Forsaken. At the time his first play was produced, in Exeter in 1878, a one-act comedietta called " Only 'Round the Corner," Mr. Jones, then twenty-seven years old, was a travelling salesman, or "bagman," for a Manchester manufacturer of stockings. " Hearts of Oak," at Exeter, and " Elopement," at Oxford, each in two acts, were others of Mr. Jones's provincial beginnings before the curtain-raiser, " A Clerical Blunder," produced by Wilson Barrett at the little Court Theatre in Chelsea in 1879, first introduced Mr. Jones to a London audience. Other one-act pieces that quickly followed were "A Bed of Roses," "An Old Master," and "Chatterton." Then Kate Bateman brought out at the Sadler's Wells Theatre Mr. Jones's first drama, "The Wife." None of his work, up to this time, had been especially successful, but its reception, nevertheless, afforded him sufficient encouragement to lead him, in 1881, to abandon trade and set up as a professional dramatist.

Mr. Jones's first big success came in 1882, when the six-act melodrama, "The Silver King," written in collaboration with Henry Herman, was produced at the Princess's Theatre by Wilson Barrett. The villain in this play was known as "The Spider," and was remarkably acted by E. S. Willard, who thereby firmly established himself in London. The melodrama displayed considerable florid rhetoric, but theatrically it was immense. In 1884, Mr. Jones had his first experience with Ibsen, whom he was instrumental in introducing into the English theatre. How little Jones understood the Scandinavian may be deduced from the fact that he and Mr. Herman, in adapting "A Doll's House" under the title of " Breaking a Butterfly," ended their version with a reconciliation between Nora and her husband. The autumn of the same year saw the production of "Saints and Sinners," the first of the characteristically Jones plays, and so uncertain was he of its acceptance by the public that in advance of its representation he tied himself up in a five years contract to write melodramas and nothing else. The results of these five years of captivity were " Hoodman Blind," " A Noble Vagabond," " The Lord Harry," " Heart of Hearts," and " Hard Hit."

" Saints and Sinners " introduced the parson into the drama, and it was Mr. Jones's first attempt to make practical a principle, which he afterward expounded in a lengthy essay, that " the drama claims for its province the whole heart and nature and soul of man." The bold annexation of an aspect of life up to that time unknown to the stage naturally caused a flurry in the " British public," which Mr. Jones is so fond of decrying. The playwright rushed into print in defence of himself and all his works, and the controversy, thus begun, has continued more or less vigorously ever since. It developed in the dramatist a burning desire to mount the forum in his plays and elucidate theories, thus, more often than not, by the injudicious union, injuring both play and theory. Thus "The Middleman" (1889) tackled the problem of capital and labour, and in "Judah" (1890), the so-called scientific spirit of the age, the give-me-provable-facts-or-I-will-not-believe spirit, was shown in contrast with the fanaticism of the religious zealot, the result being secured by the undermining of unwarranted faith in a trickster, who claimed to be able to work miracles. "The Dancing Girl" (1891); "The Crusaders" (1891), a comedy satirising hypocritical reforms, but unfortunately written with too extravagant burlesque to be entirely effective; "The Bauble Shop" (1893); "The Tempter" (1893), a tragedy in blank verse; "The Masqueraders" (1894); "The Case of Rebellious Susan" (1894), in which Mr. Jones hinted at his eternal problem by making Lady Susan Harabin run away with an emotional young man; and "The Triumph of the Philistines" (1895), all gave evidences of Mr. Jones's growing seriousness as regards sociological and religious questions, and his itching desire to make his plays a treatise on them rather than mere garnishers of public applause. Even with this handicap he was able to write financial successes, because his dramatic instinct was generally stronger than his pose as a teacher and a moralist. His plays were excellent theatrical material, and his knowledge of the stage continually stood him in good stead. Then, too,—curious paradox! —with all his ravings against the conventional morality of his " British public," Jones himself was never very far from the beaten path of stern, middle-class rectitude. He never ceased to look at life from the outside, and while the things he criticised were assuredly the outgrowths of some hidden cause, the dramatist never troubled himself greatly about the uncovering of that cause. A mocker and railer on the housetops, he was valiant in the disclosing of superficial faults, but he never advanced a method whereby these faults could be eradicated in the present and escaped in the future.

Finally, in the development of Mr. Jones's problem plays, came " Michael and His Lost

Angel," the vigour of which caused the " British public," which the dramatist had been lashing into action for so many years, to be shocked in so determined a manner that Mr. Jones's views of the function of the drama underwent a sudden and decided change. Jones has continued to kick against the pricks, it is true, but not since " Michael and His Lost Angel " has he worked the particular vein that brought about his condemnation. The keenest and the safest of English dramatic critics insisted at the time it was produced that " Michael and His Lost Angel " was Mr. Jones's masterpiece. William Archer wrote, " Mr. Jones has enriched . . . our literature with a beautiful love story." George Bernard Shaw declared, " The melancholy truth of the matter is that the English stage got a good play, and was hopelessly beaten by it." Joseph Knight went on record with, " ' Michael and His Lost Angel ' is the best play Mr. Jones has given the stage, and is in the full sense a masterpiece." Yet the drama, produced in London in January, 1896, was withdrawn after ten performances, while in New York, it failed even more decisively.

Here is indeed a contradiction. Wherein shall we find reconciliation?

I never saw the play acted, but, judging it by the unsatisfactory method of perusal of the text, " Michael and His Lost Angel " is keen, direct, uncompromising, and dramatically intense. It is also a certain shaker-up of the conventionally moral, in whose ethics the only sin that is worth repenting, or that merits punishment, is the sin that is found out. Repellant and shocking as Mr. Jones's theme may have been to the hypocritical and self-righteous, I do not believe that that was the circumstance which furnished the rock on which the play was wrecked. Wittingly or unwittingly, Mr. Jones made an attack on theological dogma that was simply not to be answered. Now theological dogma, because of the mistaken idea that it is coincident with Christianity and represents the whole of Christianity, is the religion of that vast majority which contents itself with slumbering acquiescence. To attack it as it was attacked in " Michael and His Lost Angel," always creates antagonism, all the more bitter and implacable for being partially veiled and not directly expressed. It was the silent antagonism of disturbed and perturbed thought that killed Mr. Jones's play, thought that refused to consider the question, " Can these things really be true ? "

The Reverend Michael Feversham, an austere ascetic, living under a self-imposed vow of celibacy, is Mr. Jones's representative of ecclesiasticism. Feversham regards his Church as his all. He labours and sacrifices for it, and, according to every theory of creed and dogmatic formula, his Church should be a shield and buckler to him in the warfare against temptation and sin. It proves to be nothing of the sort, however, and Feversham falls an easy, almost a willing, victim to the insinuating assault of that passion which in common parlance is termed love.

Of course, Mr. Jones has frills to his play, but with those it is not necessary to bother. The theme is as set forth, and Feversham's experience is the single essential of the plot. It is plain that, in thus dealing with ecclesiasticism, Mr. Jones spoke bluntly for the truth. There is no protection in ceremonials, though an impressionable nature may derive from them both inspiration and emotional ecstasy. But this truth, that the letter availeth nothing, is most unwelcome to all who are afraid to think, who are chiefly anxious to deceive themselves with the illusion that their future existence is all mapped out, because they have had the foresight to proclaim themselves in accord with a certain brand of theology. I think that in this fear to know the truth, lest the foundations of belief and religion be thereby shaken, reposes the reason why Mr. Jones's interesting play failed to meet popular approval. It was altogether too discommoding; it too vigorously assailed those so-called sacred things which a secretly dissatisfied world is trying with the desperation of despair to make itself believe are still valuable aids toward spirituality.

In " The Rogue's Comedy " (1896), a thoroughly excellent and a thoroughly good-natured satire, Mr. Jones found the success that was denied him in the case of " Michael and His Lost Angel," but his plays since " The Rogue's Comedy " have not shown him in quite so favourable a light. They have been smartly written, but their quality has not been much above the second rate. The list comprises "The Physician" and "The Liars" in 1897; "The Lackey's Carnival," "Carnac Sahib," and "The Goal," all of which failed; "The Manœuvres of Jane" (1899) and "Mrs. Dane's Defence" (1900).

"The Manœuvres of Jane" belonged distinctly to the order of farce, though, probably, the dramatist intended to write a satirical comedy, even if he did get no farther on the way than to provide a first act of comedy pretensions. He introduced, in rapid succession, an entertaining lot of characters, and developed an action that was full of surprises, and comparatively free from explanations. After exploiting a straight situation in this act, however, and pairing off his four lovers before the play was fairly under way, thus settling then and there what would naturally have formed the main complications of his plot, Mr. Jones really had no plot development left for the last two acts of his play. Amusing incidents there were in abundance, but the comedy degenerated into a farce both superficial and artificial. Mr. Jones's play simply brought about the long anticipated. One knew from the beginning that the sly and scheming Constantia would somehow or other worm a proposal of marriage from the self-satisfied and easily worked Lord Bapchild. One knew that the pretty and wilful and sharp-tempered Jane would surely bring her peppery papa to terms, and finally marry young Langdon, the man of her choice.

"Mrs. Dane's Defence" was better drama than Mr. Jones had written for many seasons. It presented an unusual type of the woman with a past. The dramatist, with the quickening aid of a delicately human touch that was not felt in the moulding of any other character in the play, delineated an adventuress who was neither repulsively bold in her vaunting wickedness nor sickeningly plaintive in her remorseful repentance. Even after one had waded with her through a morass of lies and deceptions, one believed her thoroughly when she cried, in the agony of her shame and mental anguish, "I am not a bad woman;" and he granted her the absolution which is the due — in plays and in books, even if not in real life — of the woman who has been sinned against. Nevertheless, although she does compel compassion because of her wrongs, Mrs. Dane differs decidedly from the usual run of the "sinned-againsts" of the stage. She does not indulge in the customary mental flutter of protest, and she does not meekly succumb to the verdict of ostracism. She fights back with refreshing vigour, though her weapons of guile and deceit are of a distinctly inferior order. Well-nigh distracted by the burden of fear, still she fights back desperately, hopelessly, till her poor armour of lies is pierced again and again, till, stricken with bitterness to the very heart, she is prostrate at the feet of the man who, with his torturing questions, has at last dragged the shameful truth from her.

An interesting problem in ethics is illustrated by Mrs. Dane, a problem which, I am quite sure, Mr. Jones, who talks so diffusely and indefinitely about some sort of a law that makes Mrs. Dane's punishment just, as well as inevitable, by no means intelligently comprehends. In support of his inexorable law, Mr. Jones advances an unconvincing argument, for the simple reason that he does not himself honestly believe what he is trying to prove.

JESSIE MILLWARD AND CHARLES RICHMAN
In " Mrs. Dane's Defence "

Although he stands sturdily to his self-imposed task of upholding with stern morality the bulwarks of society, although he blusters and blows mightily in the effort to conceal the embarrassing personal equation that is presented in the woman herself, he assuredly feels from the ground up that society is acting the part of the bigot in condemning utterly the unfortunate woman. To strengthen his case against her, he piles on more and still more disaster, adds suicide and insanity to her account, after those a child, and finally a mountain of lies. Even then his sympathy remains with Lady Eastney, Mrs. Dane's champion, and not with Lady Bulsom-Porter, her traducer. No, Mr. Jones does not by any means second the high-sounding opinion regarding the moral law that he puts into the mouth of Sir Daniel Carteret, his spokesman. The dramatist argues against his own convictions. His words are insincere, and consequently they carry no weight. Did the success of the drama depend upon their acceptance as truth, Mr. Jones's structure would quickly tumble about his head, a veritable house of cards.

Yet, Mr. Jones was right in making Mrs.

Dane give up the young man whom she loved so deeply and who was so ready and so anxious to marry her in spite of scandal and all else. Sir Daniel was right, too, in his declaration that marriage in that case — no matter how great the mutual affection and how deeply rooted the passion — would have surely led to unhappiness and ultimate distrust and separation. Moreover, Mrs. Dane's punishment — the loss both of reputation and the man she loved — was just, even as it was inevitable. In short, the conclusions that Mr. Jones arrived at in his play were wholly correct, but his arguments in support of them were wholly wrong. If only he had not made Sir Daniel utter such foolish platitudes! If only he had been content to let Mrs. Dane, as a fully developed dramatic conception, speak for herself! Or, if he felt compelled bluntly to deduce a moral, why did he not point out the higher truth — that the woman's fault of ignorance was fully atoned for by the loss of the material blessings of a good name and an honest man's love and esteem and protection, but that, because she had been more sinned against than sinning, because she was not vicious, but unfortunate, her woman's nature was in its finer essentials untarnished; that the bud of loveliness of character had not been absolutely blasted, and was still capable of quickly expanding into the full bloom of fragrant richness; and that her true self, when nurtured by patiently endured suffering, would surely bring forth an eternal fruitage of purity, tenderness, and heroic sacrifice?

It was the dramatist's earnest insistence, in his development of the part, on Mrs. Dane's underlying womanliness that made the character one of much subtle interest. As the play grew, one saw the inherent nobility of the woman come slowly into view. It was as the gradual uncovering of a beautiful statue, which had been long swathed into ugly shapelessness by uncouth wrappings. When, finally stripped of every disfiguring evil, the pure gold of her unselfish love was revealed, Mr. Jones had completed a study of character both truthful and inspiring, a study the deep helpfulness of which was not to be destroyed even by its originator's unfortunate misconceptions regarding it.

As for the construction of the play, " Mrs.

Dane's Defence," one cannot forbear the suggestion that Mr. Jones learned his Arthur Wing Pinero very well indeed. "The Gay Lord Quex" was produced in London on April 8, 1899. "Mrs. Dane's Defence" was produced in the same city on October 9, 1900. I would not be so discourteous as to hint that Mr. Jones consciously modelled his work after Mr. Pinero's skilful production, and, indeed, as regards theme, characters, plot, — every detail, in fact, — the two dramas were wholly dissimilar. But in workmanship, in technique, in artificiality of construction, they were strikingly alike. One received from "Mrs. Dane's Defence" precisely the same impression of mechanical perfection without convincing reality that he received from "The Gay Lord Quex." In both instances one felt, a trifle resentfully, that his emotions had been the playthings of accomplished jugglers.

There was this much difference between the two. Mr. Jones's machinery was not quite so carefully oiled as was Mr. Pinero's. Mr. Pinero's "big scene" — the wonderful combat between Lord Quex and Sophy Fullgarney — was breathless throughout in its intensity

and suspense. Mr. Jones's "big scene"—
wherein, by means of his relentless cross-ques-
tioning, Sir Daniel Carteret brought to bay
the lying Mrs. Dane—did drag in spots,
thereby driving the spectator into a condition
of nervous irritability. One perceived that
Mr. Jones was constantly applying the brake.
In his anxiety to attain the superlative of
effect, he slightly overdeveloped his situations,
retarded his climaxes by excessive prolonging
of the suspense, laboured too strenuously for
the important element of contrast. It is quite
true that when at length the final grand rush
to the supreme climax did come, it was quite
irresistible and overwhelming, but how Mr.
Jones did back and fill before he got there!

CHAPTER III.

N addition to Mr. Pinero and Mr. Jones there are a few more than half a dozen English dramatists, who write regularly for the stage, and have gained especial favour thereon. Among this number one can scarcely include George Bernard Shaw, whose genius for placing himself on the other side of things, and whose deliberate and erratic perverseness preclude the possibility of taking him seriously, even as a protest. If Shaw only had the faintest notion of the meaning of sincerity, he would be an interesting phenomenon. But he is not to be trusted, either as a clown or as a philosopher.

Representative of modern artificial comedy, the direct descendant of Sheridan, is R. C. Carton, whose "Lord and Lady Algy," "Wheels within Wheels," and "Lady Huntworth's Experiment" all have the snap, the

As Richard Carewe in " When We Were Twenty-one."

sparkle, the glitter, and the polish of well-wrought wit. H. V. Esmond has penetrated a little deeper, for, after failing with an Ibsenish drama, "Grierson's Way," and with a light comedy, "One Summer's Day," he presented, in "When We Were Twenty-One," a comedy of fine flavour, well-formed character, and definite purpose. Captain R. Marshall, who made his first flight in a fantastic, farcical affair not without its fascinations, "His Excellency the Governor," and then invaded fairy-land with a pretty conceit, "A Royal Family," touched life with far more certainty in "The Second in Command." Sydney Grundy, who has spent his time since 1872 dashing back and forth between original work and adaptations, was last heard from in "The Degenerates," a comedy of some problem interest. C. Haddon Chambers, who used to be called "the boy dramatist" when his melodramatic "Captain Swift" was a fresh sensation, has given an entertaining comedy study of femininity in "The Tyranny of Tears," and Leo Trevor, a newcomer, has been surprisingly successful with his "Brother Officers," a comedy of character with a moving theme somewhat crudely elaborated and manœuvred. Louis N. Parker, like Sydney Grundy, more successful as an adapter than as an originator, flew ambitious flights none too well with "The Cardinal," while Justin Huntly McCarthy, labouring in the same romantic field, secured, with "If I Were King," precisely the effect of idealised reality that Mr. Parker missed.

Recently, moreover, various novelists have attempted the drama with varying results. The most consistent performer has been J. M. Barrie, whose "The Little Minister" (nominally a dramatisation of a novel, but in effect an original play), "The Professor's Love Story," and "Quality Street" have united quaint charm with positive merit. John Oliver Hobbes (Mrs. Craigie) has written an unusually brilliant comedy, if one confine himself to the reading of it, in "The Ambassador." Unfortunately, on the stage it proved a bloodless and artificial thing. Jerome K. Jerome came nearer the mark by translating his peculiar brand of humour for the theatre in "Miss Hobbs," which amply sufficed as an entertainment.

From this list of plays, ranging from the

meritorious to the inconsequential, a half a dozen have been selected for closer examination. They are not necessarily the best six plays, but they are six that are fairly representative of the lot. The dramas chosen are Justin Huntly McCarthy's " If I Were King," Louis N. Parker's " The Cardinal," J. M. Barrie's " Quality Street," Captain R. Marshall's " The Second in Command," R. C. Carton's "Lady Huntworth's Experiment," and Sydney Grundy's " The Degenerates."

" If I Were King," in which Edward H. Sothern created François Villon, being both interesting and imaginative, may without exaggeration be termed the most worthy and the most directly successful essay in the habiliment of the romantic drama in English that has been recorded for years. As a literary drama — the word literary being used in the restricted sense of "readable "—it would seem thoroughly excellent. As an acting drama it fully meets the test. It provides characters in whose fortunes and sayings one is really concerned; action—a vital element in a play, for without it there can be nought either to fix the attention or to colour the emotions — that is pointedly interesting ; colour, contrast, picturesqueness, and atmosphere that casts a glamour of mystery and romance without actually destroying the sense of reality, things that are all of them valuable accessories without any one of them being absolute necessities.

In dealing with the vagabond poet of France of the fifteenth century, Mr. McCarthy did not choose wholly novel material, for other dramas have dallied in the same fertile pastures. However, that fact bears not a feather's weight against the contention that Mr. McCarthy has written the François Villon play of his day and generation. This character, so full of light and shade, of pure idealism and debasing filthiness, is dramatic without the touch of the dramatist. François Villon — to use the name by which he is known in literature, though in life he had as many aliases as a cat has lives — was born in 1431 and died in 1461, or thereabouts. In 1455 came the first important incident of his life, so far as is known, a fight with a priest named Philippe Sermaiée, who was so severely wounded by Villon that he died. Villon was

EDWARD H. SOTHERN
As François Villon in "If I Were King"

banished from Paris, but was pardoned six months later. A year after that, Katherine de Vancelles, of whom quite frequent mention is made in Villon's poems, was the cause of a second quarrel, which brought Villon such a flogging that in very shame he left the city. During his absence he was accused of robbing a church, arrested on his return, tortured, and sentenced to be hanged. This was, however, commuted to banishment. Four years then passed without tidings of Villon, but when Louis XI. ascended the throne in 1461, the poet was again in jail, being one of those released therefrom by royal clemency at the time of the coronation. The time and the manner of Villon's end are not known, but his death probably occurred not long after this last experience.

In his play Mr. McCarthy utilised as one the two separate episodes of the fight with the priest and the row in which Katherine de Vancelles was in some way mixed up. The main incident of the drama — the transforming in a single night of the vagabond Villon into the mighty head constable of the kingdom — was, of course, wholly fictional, the free borrowing of a situation hoary with antiquity. It was also distinctly an anachronism to bring together a Louis XI. in his dotage and a Villon in the full bloom of youth, for Louis was born in 1823, and Villon only eight years after that. These points are not made in the way of faultfinding, but simply as interesting details in connection with a drama that is likely to be acted for some time longer than a single season.

By leaving history largely out of consideration, Mr. McCarthy succeeded in drawing a François Villon that ranked well up in the gallery of modern dramatic conceptions. Both Mr. McCarthy's play and his character suggest Edmond Rostand's "Cyrano de Bergerac," and I am not so sure that the Englishman is not entitled to the credit of having beaten the Frenchman on his own ground. Certainly, "If I Were King" is a more homogeneous work than "Cyrano de Bergerac." "Cyrano" is strictly the setting forth of a single character, and everything is sacrificed and subordinated to that character. Strained situations are created for the sole purpose of enabling that character to shine, and a conclusion is reached that, while it is intensely moving, is nevertheless wholly arbitrary.

In " If I Were King," Villon is well blended into the general scheme. He is always first, but he is never alone. In the brawling tavern scene of the first act — a conventional situation so ingeniously treated as to seem actually novel — he is part, not the whole, of the action. That strong conception, Huguette du Hamel, mockingly called the Abbess, woman of the town who brazenly wears the apparel of a man that she may the better show her fine shape, so she says, — a conception that almost the turn of a phrase might change into a bubble of sentimentality, — during the early moments of this act shares the interest with Villon, as later does the King and the haughty Katherine, with her demand for the death of an obnoxious rival at the hands of the poor poet, who has dared to speak of love to her. This dividing of the interest is still maintained in the second act, when the plan of the crafty King, to use Villon both to fight France's foes and to wreak the petty royal vengeance on a woman, is disclosed. For a week the command of France's army is in Villon's hands. In that time the clamorous Duke of Burgundy must be conquered and the cold Katherine must be wooed and won, if Villon would save his neck. Thus on poet and King and fair lady the action is finally centred.

At first, all is serene for the poet. He proves himself a man come to court, and love is his. So, too, the King's enemies fall before him, and power is his. But the King clouds the sun with a dark shadow. How will the lady like the deception? Will she take for her husband a poor poet whom she has imagined to be a high-born noble? The test is made, and the poet is entirely undone. Pride speaks before love, and the gibbet, gloomy sentinel over the merrymaking and victorious rejoicings of the returned soldiers, which ushers in the last act, is a prophecy of the end of François Villon. Almost to the foot of the gallows Mr. McCarthy continues without a drop the keen interest in the outcome of his plot. Then, it must be confessed, the situation floors him. It is a choice between hanging a poet and marrying him off. The dramatist decides on marriage, which would be right and proper and eminently satisfactory, were it not that he delays a trifle too long in getting to the end, after he has made the end plain. Thus the final curtain is smothered in an anticlimax.

Many especial points of beauty are to be found in the drama. One such is the really remarkable entrance of Villon in the second act, while he is still bewildered beyond comprehension by his fine surroundings, and before he understands why he, François Villon, should be bowed down to as a great noble. Another is the interview between Villon and Katherine in this same act — love voiced by him, the demand from her for a man to save France. Again there is the contrast so clearly shown between the Abbess, moved by an affection maternal in its unselfishness, and the Abbess instantly thereafter changed into a wanton. Finally, as the crowning glory of the drama, there is the beautiful scene in the third act depicting the triumph of the poet in the love of his fair lady. This scene, so chaste, so ideal, so genuinely inspiring, is the worthy apex of an exceptionally fine play.

"THE CARDINAL"

Louis N. Parker's play, "The Cardinal," which Edward S. Willard acted in the United States during the season of 1901–02, experimented with the same theatricalism from which Bulwer-Lytton wrought his fine acting play "Richelieu." "The Cardinal" was distinctly a spectacular and romantic melodrama, and Mr. Willard blundered when he failed to take advantage of this fact, and stage the play in a spectacular manner. The drama demanded above all else a crowd; it required seething multitudes, the clamour and the picturesqueness of the mob, the theatrical thrill that is inspired by a vast concourse of people emotionally moved. "The Cardinal" belonged to the purely formal in a theatrical classification. Acted quietly and simply, it could not avoid being artificial, forced, and impossible, but given a setting both eye and ear compelling, it might have been numbered among the distinct successes.

By placing his action in Rome in 1510, and by developing his plot almost within the portals of the Vatican, even going so far as to use the sanctity of the Roman Catholic confession as the motive-force of his story, Mr. Parker gained for his play a telling environment, inherent interest, and suggestive possibilities. The locale was of itself dramatic. However, he subjected himself, by not choosing the ready haven of comedy, to the necessity either of writing a moving poetic drama, or else of following Bulwer-Lytton's consistent example, and bringing forth a romantic melodrama of striking, even though unconvincing, intrigue. Possibly Mr. Parker, who is not without poetical aspirations, tried his best to achieve glowing romanticism. Mr. Willard's subdued presentation of the piece hinted that such was the case. But, if the dramatist did intend a stirring and inspiring appeal to the imagination, he missed his purpose, and, by doing so, impaled himself on the second horn of the dilemma. Instead of poetic idealism, he dealt out four acts of promising theatricalism and spectacular opportunities.

Indeed, can you picture any situation inherently less real, and yet more intensely theatric, than the one embodied in Mr. Parker's play? There is the magic potency of Rome at a time when one fancies that almost any impossible thing may happen. There is a cardinal in bright red, who, after listening to a murderer's confession, permits his own brother, convicted on circumstantial evidence of the identical murder, to advance to the scaffold because he, the cardinal, is lip-sealed by the confessional. Then, at the last instant, and after the last drop of agony has been extracted from the situation, behold this self-same cardinal save his brother by trapping the real murderer into a revelation of his crime within the hearing of concealed witnesses! Of course, there is a beautiful woman betrothed to the brother and greatly desired by the murderer, complicating the motive, and adding her share to the suspense and the emotional tension. In fact, there is everything except sincerity, truth, and honest art. Of these promoters of genuine emotion, there is not a vestige, and, consequently, the whole structure falls flat.

"QUALITY STREET"

Back in the days of Waterloo, though neither a Wellington nor a Napoleon ap-

MAUDE ADAMS

As Phœbe in "Quality Street"

peared on the stage, J. M. Barrie placed his odd little play, "Quality Street," in which Maude Adams appeared for the first time in the fall of 1901. The adjective quaint is the single one distinctly applicable to everything about this play. It applies to Mr. Barrie's theme, his characters, his method of illustrating customs and manners, his humour, and his idea of how a play should be made. Mr. Barrie knows very well what he wants a play to be, but, as regards how to reveal his idea in dramatic form, his notions are — call them quaint, for that is a comparatively harmless word. There is enough brilliant material, delicate conceit, rich and characteristic humour, moving sentiment, and pathos in "Quality Street" to make a comedy of abiding literary and dramatic worth. Unfortunately, considerable of this splendid material is wasted, solely because Mr. Barrie lacks thorough understanding of theatrical workmanship.

Even with its failings, however, "Quality Street" is a very entertaining play, having always in evidence Mr. Barrie's ingratiating sympathy, his sweet appreciation of the tender, the true, and the pure in human nature, and his fine balance between laughter and tears. These exceptionally winsome factors give tone and vitality to the drama. They make it interesting, even when it fails to be incisive. Could there be a more enticing portrayal of the old-fashioned ideal of feminine modesty and gentility than in the first act of "Quality Street?" It was the atmosphere of Cranford dramatised!—precise, unsophisticated Susan with her own poor, pathetic romance cherished carefully in her memory; the prying trio of self-depreciating, self-satisfied, gossipy, old-young women, "females," as they called themselves; Betty, the perfect embodiment of the servant, who is not only one of the family, but who is the real boss of the family as well; little Phœbe herself, she of the ringlets, whose prettiness is going to win for her that strange but desirable commodity of which the others have sometimes wildly dreamed, though for which they never have actually dared to hope,—a husband!

Although it was old England about which Mr. Barrie wrote, I could not help bringing that first act over into New England. Whenever a window was opened I smelled the east wind. I have seen Miss Susan in the flesh, and I think that she taught school, too; and modest little Phœbe also, foolish, modest Phœbe, who tortured herself and tried her very best to make herself old and ugly, because she had let the man she loved kiss her, and because he has gone away to the wars without saying in so many words that he loved her and was going to marry her. It is a wonderful first act in its quiet, peaceful, natural, unassuming way, the very quintessence of high-class comedy.

None of the other three acts reached quite so high, though throughout Mr. Barrie maintained with vividness and fidelity his exceptionally fine studies of character. Where he lost was in the securing of perfect conviction and in projecting throughout the play the atmosphere so perfectly attained in the first act. As his comedy became more shallow, less dependent on character, less illustrative of manners, it broadened and coarsened almost to the verge of farce. It is true that pathos was never far away, but there were times when one had to analyse rather closely to find it. If one recalled the Phœbe of the first act and compared her with the worn schoolma'am Phœbe of the second act, the underlying tragedy was apparent. But it took quite a bit of thought to make such a comparison. It was much easier to laugh at the schoolchildren and at Phœbe's ineffectual efforts to discipline them. In these and analogous situations Mr. Barrie's imperfect estimate of theatrical effect betrayed itself, nor was this imperfection at all tempered by staging the play with a bluntness that emphatically demanded a loud laugh. Mr. Barrie's purpose was to mingle laughter with tears by contrasting the Phœbe of the first act with the Phœbe of the second, but he forgot that what one sees before him on the stage counts for much more than what he remembers that he saw. The result was Mr. Barrie got only laughter, the zest of which was lost in a feeling that for some reason or other this laughter was neither polite nor charitable.

"THE SECOND IN COMMAND"

John Drew presented Captain Robert Marshall's four-act comedy, "The Second in Command," and the play proved an exceedingly interesting one, going a long way toward veri-fying the assertion that it was the best play that Mr. Drew had had since he began starring. Certainly the leading character provided Mr. Drew with an excellent quality of the brand of acting that he has made his specialty. Without going so far as to rank Captain Marshall anywhere near Mr. Pinero, or even the uncertain Mr. Jones, in constructive ability and thorough theatrical effectiveness, it is, never-theless, only just to give him warm com-mendation for a sincerity and an idealism in character conception that are as grateful as they are unusual. One does not have to seek long in order to find flaws in the technical de-tails of Captain Marshall's work. His heroine's extraordinary premonition that something is going to happen at the end of the first act is one. This same Muriel's nonchalant method of put-ting off the old love and putting on the new is another. " Kit's " oddly motived lie, on which the plot is so vitally dependent, is a third. This lie cannot, from the dramatist's expo-sition of the case, be defended, while the anticlimax of the medal episode of the last act is not permissible in any playwright unless his reputation for infallibility be positively Shakespearian.

Yet none of these obvious structural deformities weighs much against the success of the comedy, for the sufficient reason that Captain Marshall has peopled his scenes with real men and women, whose motives, actions, sentiments, sufferings, joys, and sorrows are understandable and genuine. Without gliding off into sermonising on the one side, or into the impregnable virtue of priggish snow-whiteness on the other, " The Second in Command " still succeeds in giving one a decided hoist upward. It furnishes one in a small way with an honest inspiration. It is really worth while. Moreover, it has, too, an abundance of wit in the turn of its lines, some positive humour in its situations, and moments when its pathos is true enough to dampen the eyelashes.

In writing an English military play, Captain Marshall had the advantage of dealing with atmosphere with which he was thoroughly familiar, and he depicted army life somewhat as it is, and not entirely as the average stage-manager thinks that it should be. The plot of " The Second in Command," simple enough in dramatic form, would be complicated and cumbrous in the telling. It is enough to know that the story is woven around the complicated love-affairs of Muriel Mannering, a poor girl with a brother in the army and in debt. Muriel lives with Lady Harburgh, who tried to be kind, but who acts otherwise. She is continually telling Muriel to hurry up and get married, in order to escape her own poverty and to cease being a burden on her friends. Under this stress the young woman accepts the offer of Major Bingham, who has for some time been in the habit of proposing to her annually. Then, having thus disposed of her future, Muriel proceeds to fall in love with the handsome and rich Lieutenant-Colonel Anstruther, — an exceedingly expeditious process, which takes place in full view of the audience and forms the none too convincing conclusion of the first act. Having made so much mischief, Muriel bungles matters still worse in the second act, by telling poor Bingham that she cannot be his wife and promising Anstruther that she will marry him. Now these unconscious rivals are the best of friends, and they continue the best of friends throughout the play. Naturally they compare notes, and Anstruther reaches the conclusion that Muriel is after him for his money, which will be useful just then in settling the pressing debts of Muriel's brother. He argues that, having been engaged to Bingham, she must love him, and that she threw Bingham over because of his impoverished exchequer.

Then follows Anstruther's momentous question, put to Bingham, "Does she love you?" Bingham knows that she does not, and he knows, too, that Anstruther loves her. What he does not know is exactly how Muriel feels toward Anstruther. He thinks that possibly she would marry the colonel to save her brother. Justifying himself with the plea that "All's fair in love and war," Bingham lies. He answers that Muriel does love him. Thereupon Anstruther calls everything off between himself and Muriel. Of course, it is necessary for the furtherance of Captain Marshall's plot that Bingham should lie at that particular point, but there should be some way to make him lie without meanness, for meanness is not in accordance with his character as it is drawn by the dramatist. The lie that Bingham does lie is, as a matter of fact, an outrageous libel on a good fellow. It cannot for a moment be countenanced. Suppose, for instance, that Bingham thought that Muriel was being forced into a marriage distasteful to her, and that he lied with the chivalrous intent of saving her? That, it would seem, might have accomplished the purpose, and at the same time have kept Bingham's character straight, and thereby strengthened the play.

"LADY HUNTWORTH'S EXPERIMENT"

"Lady Huntworth's Experiment," a three-act comedy by R. C. Carton, was acted in this country by Daniel Frohman's Company from Daly's New York Theatre, Hilda Spong appearing in the title part. After one has summed up the impression created by the play with the plain statement that Mr. Carton has written an exceedingly light, but a thoroughly entertaining comedy, he has with this deserved compliment practically uttered the last word. There is almost nothing to discuss about "Lady Huntworth's Experiment," no especial brilliancy about which to weave ecstasies, and no dreadful blemishes over which to moan. Nor is the play so commonplace as these conditions might indicate. It is, in fact, plain, easy sailing from the rise of the curtain to the fall, and the whole duty of the happy one out front in the audience is accomplished in the pleasant task of thoroughly enjoying himself.

After inserting the qualifying clause that light comedy has its privileges, and that its incongruities are to be accepted without undue questioning, if only they bring with them justifying merriment, it may be declared that Mr. Carton's scheme of placing a society woman in the position of cook in the modest household of a country clergyman, has, as a conception, the distinct merit of suggestive comedy contrast — a contrast that is somewhat above the broadly farcical, in that it provides ample opportunity for illustrating and developing character through the mediumship of action. That Mr. Carton attained quite the maximum of effect which his original conception suggested, I am not so sure, but he attained

HILDA SPONG

As Lady Huntworth in " Lady Huntworth's Experiment "

enough to answer his immediate purposes. There was fascination in the way in which he played the fondness of the suave and wordy vicar for the cook, against the honest, blunt, undisguised, and thoroughly manly affection of Captain Dorvaston for the same charmer; and there was delicate satire in placing both of these swains in rivalry with the decidedly businesslike love of the portentous Gandy, a butler whose worldly ambition fixed its pinnacle on a " h'eatin'-'ouse " that could be purchased on the instalment plan.

The introduction of Lady Huntworth's husband, with his delirium tremens, his spiders, and his thoroughly disgusting caddishness, was to me the one jarring element in the play. The unwholesomeness of the character seemed out of touch with the spirit of the work as a whole, and, moreover, its specific setting forth on the stage served no very convincing purpose. The part gave nothing that could not have been indicated by a less shocking and horrifying portrayal of depravity. The character, indeed, struck me as more of a sensational melodrama villain than as an example of the plain, ordinary, every-day sort of villainy, which, unexaggerated, is earnest enough for easy-going light comedy.

"THE DEGENERATES"

Sydney Grundy's "The Degenerates," in which Mrs. Langtry played Mrs. Trevelyan, was an unusual mixture of exceptional strength and commonplace weakness, a condition which was due to a tendency to drift into conventional melodrama, not so much in situation, perhaps,—though melodrama was by no means far distant at certain periods in the third act, —as in the literary style of some of the dialogue. Mr. Grundy most inartistically mixed with free, easy, and slangy speeches — talk quite in keeping with several of his characters — stilted periods that were reminiscent of the dramatic style of fifty years before. Now Mr. Grundy's chief element of strength was his character-drawing; and the effect of personages, who had enough of the attributes of the modern man and woman to make them seem real, speaking blank-verse language, was singularly incongruous. I should make a guess that the trouble was the fault, mainly, of hasty and careless composition.

The story of " The Degenerates " did not strike one who listened to its telling on the stage as particularly far - fetched. Yet, in thinking it over, one perceived that some of its episodes were, to say the least, not in the every-day experience of the every-day individual. Lady Samaurez, the jealous woman, who, loving her husband, thinks to avenge herself for his unfaithfulness by running away with the most convenient man; Sir William, the recreant husband, and Isidore De Lorano, the most convenient man, were all the ordinary lay figures of melodrama. But the Duke of Orme, man of the world, idealist, and accurate judge of human nature, gave one something new to think about; and Mrs. Trevelyan, too, was full of substance, a character the possibilities of which in the way of dramatic treatment were only hinted at. Looking at the character in any light one pleased,—as a woman reformed by love, as one of those inexplicable creatures whose strong personality will not endure the confines of social convention, or as a human being totally misunderstood and misjudged, —one could not escape its fascination.

The woman was paradoxical but she was human.

Recognise this human quality in Mrs. Trevelyan, and one readily perceives why Mr. Grundy's situations seemed in the passing so very probable, or, to put it still stronger, so almost inevitable. Mrs. Trevelyan explained them. For her, that impulsive sacrifice of reputation to save another woman, though that woman had done her a mean turn, was possible; in any other woman it would have been inexplicable and absurd. Mr. Grundy, moreover, was aided in the exposition of this character by the biographical flavour given the part through the narration of certain incidents in Mrs. Trevelyan's career that suggested parallel incidents in the career of the actress who impersonated Mrs. Trevelyan. The spectator was unquestionably led to identify Mrs. Langtry with Mrs. Trevelyan, and this identification undoubtedly had a definite effect in vitalising the conception.

CHAPTER IV.

N April, 1786, the first American drama to receive a production by a regular company of professional play-ers was acted in New York. It was a five-act comedy called " The Contrast," and its author was Royall Tyler (1758–1826), who was born in Boston, was graduated from Harvard, studied law with John Adams, fought in the Revolution, and died chief justice of the Supreme Court of Vermont. In his " History of the American Stage," William Dunlap described this play as deficient in plot, dialogue, and incident, though he declared that it showed some marking in character. What is chiefly interesting about it is the fact that the first American play to be acted should have been responsible for the introduction into the theatre of the stage Yankee, for Tyler's Jonathan was the forgotten father of all the Asa Trenchards, the Solon Shingles, the Bardwell Slotes, and the Joshua Whitcombs that have come after. Whatever its faults may have been, " The Contrast " met with fair favour, and its author was encouraged to bring out, shortly after, " May Day, or New York in an Uproar," a farce, and " The Georgia Spec, or Land in the Moon," a three-act comedy.

Although Tyler's plays were the first acted, Thomas Godfrey, Jr. (1736–63), son of the inventor of the quadrant, is usually called the first American dramatist, but, like the works of many American dramatists since his time, his tragedy, " Prince of Parthia," failed to get a production. It was offered to a theatrical company playing in Philadelphia, but it was not accepted. To vindicate himself, Godfrey had it printed and published in Philadelphia. Before Tyler appeared on the scene, Barnabas Bidwell (1763–1833), a Massachusetts man, and the son of a minister, a graduate from Yale in 1785, who received an LL. D. from Brown in 1805, and who died in Kingston, Canada, whither he had fled after robbing a bank in his native State, also wrote a tragedy, — " a very pleasant and laughter-provoking tragedy," William Dunlap termed it, — the name of which was " The Mercenary Match." It was acted by Yale students, and published in New Haven in 1785.

The most important of these early dramatists, however, was William Dunlap himself, " the father of the American stage," the founder of the American Academy of Design, and the man whom the Dunlap Society of New York delights to honour. He was born in Perth Amboy, New Jersey, on February 19, 1766, and died in New York on September 28, 1839. Dunlap went to New York in 1777, and there he studied painting. In 1784 he crossed over to London, and during his three years' stay in that city became greatly interested in the theatre. His first play, " The Modest Soldier, or Love in New York," was written directly after his return to New York, but it was never acted, although accepted for production at the John Street Theatre. His first work to be seen by the public was " The Father, or American Shandyism," played in 1789. This was also the first American play to be both acted and printed. In 1796 Dunlap became connected with the management of the John Street Theatre in New York, and the next season he was given the sole management of the new Park Theatre in that city. There he tried to establish a home for the American drama, but this attempt to put art before business landed him in the bankruptcy court in 1805. Dunlap was a prolific writer of plays, ranging in almost infinite variety from tragedy to farce. There is a record of about sixty-five of his dramatic works, and there may have been a number more, for Dunlap parcelled the manuscripts out among managers, and doubtless many were lost. Dunlap's first tragedy, " The Fatal Deception, or the Progress of Guilt," published under the title of " Lord Leicester," was the " first American tragedy performed by professed players." It lasted only through a few representations, and Dunlap confessed that "as a tragedy, it was justly doomed to oblivion." The best known of Dunlap's plays is the five-act tragedy, " André," acted in 1798, which, together with " The Father," has been published by the Dunlap Society.

From the first of the century until about 1830, when Edwin Forrest began to offer prizes for American plays, the prejudice against the native dramatist was strong enough summarily to damn any play the authorship of which was ascribed to an American. That some of these American plays were intrinsically good enough to suit the popular taste of the time was proved by James Nelson Barker (1784–1858), whose " Marmion, or the Battle of Flodden," a dramatisation of Scott's poem, was enthusiastically received after it had judicially been announced as "the great London success by Thomas Morton." John Howard Payne (1791–1852) was the only American dramatist to attain an acknowledged standing during this period, and he made his reputation in London, and from that vantage-ground successfully invaded the American theatre. Payne was exceedingly precocious, and his first play, a five-act comedy called " Julia, or the Wanderer," was acted in New York in 1806, when the dramatist was only fifteen years old. Payne made his début as an actor at the Park Theatre, New York, in 1809, playing Young Norval. Four years later he went to London, where he remained until 1832. Payne's best known play, " Brutus, or the Fall of Tarquin," was produced in the

Drury Lane Theatre in 1818, and two years after was seen in New York. Payne wrote nineteen plays in all.

Forrest's first prize offer of five hundred dollars was awarded to John Augustus Stone for his drama in verse, " Metamora." Stone was an actor, and was born in Concord, Massachusetts, in 1801. He committed suicide in 1834 by drowning himself in the Schuylkill River near Philadelphia. In 1825 he wrote a play called " Restoration, or the Diamond Cross," and the success of " Metamora " induced Forrest to produce plays of his called " The Ancient Briton " and " Fauntleroy, the Banker of Rome," but neither of them amounted to much. Stone was also the author of Yankee Hill's famous success, " The Knight of the Golden Fleece." " Metamora " was an Indian play, and was one of a long line of dramatic horrors in which the American aborigines figured as leading attractions. The earliest of these affairs was a semi-musical effort called " Tammany," written by Anne Kemble Hatton, sister of John Philip Kemble and Mrs. Sarah Siddons, and acted in New York in 1794. James N. Barker was responsible for the next

Indian play, which dealt with Pocahontas and was called "The Indian Princess." It was acted at the Park Theatre in New York in 1808. This, too, had musical numbers. George Washington Parke Custis made a second play on the same subject, which was given in New York in 1830. The best one of the lot was Robert Owen Dale's "Pocahontas," acted in 1838. The Indian invasion lasted till about 1846, when the public arose in wrath, and with unanimity hissed the noble red man from the stage.

Besides "Metamora," Forrest's attention to the American drama resulted in the production of "The Gladiator" by Robert Montgomery Bird in 1831, and in the popularising of Robert Taylor Conrad's " Aylmere, or the Bondman of Kent," afterward called " Jack Cade," in which Forrest first appeared in 1839. Charles Kean also tried an American tragedy during his first visit to this country in the early thirties, John J. Bailey's "Waldimar" being acted by him a few times in New York and Philadelphia. Both Robert Montgomery Bird (1803–54) and Robert Taylor Conrad (1810–58) lived in Philadelphia. Bird was something of a novelist, his most widely read story having been "Nick of the Woods" (1837), which was dramatised by Miss L. H. Medina. Bird's plays, in addition to "The Gladiator," were "The Broker of Bogota" and "Oraooza," neither of which was successful on the stage. Conrad was a lawyer by profession, and he served Philadelphia as mayor in 1854. His first play was "Conrad of Naples," a tragedy, which was produced at the Arch Street Theatre, Philadelphia, in 1832, by James E. Murdoch. The drama was afterward used by John R. Scott. "Jack Cade" was originally written for A. A. Addams, who appeared in it in 1835, and failed. Conrad rewrote the play for Forrest, changing the name from "The Noble Yeoman" to "Aylmere, or the Bondman of Kent," and later still to "Jack Cade."

It was an unfortunate fact that Forrest's efforts had no appreciable effect in reducing the antipathy toward the native drama, nor was the quality of the work of the native dramatist perceptibly improved. Until the comedy "Fashion," by that extraordinary woman, Anna Cora Mowatt, was brought out in 1845, all was darkness and stagnation as far as the American drama was concerned. As showing the sentiment of the times, the prologue by Epes Sargent, with which "Fashion" was fortified on the night of its production, is most suggestive. In it the audience is besought not to condemn the play before they hear it, just because it does not bear a London endorsement or because it is written by a woman. In this especial case, however, the precautionary prologue proved unnecessary, for the comedy was good enough to win out on its merits. It was distinctly fresh and original, and it had to do with contemporaneous fads and foibles. It pictured and mildly satirised the social life of the time and of the country in a manner novel to the stage and delightful to the audience. The popularity of "Fashion" lasted for some time, —as long, in fact, as the conditions that gave it point continued. Although now wholly forgotten, "Fashion" was decidedly epoch-marking. It was without doubt the best American play that had been written up to that time, and, moreover, by striking off on new lines, by abandoning the melodramatic, the formal, and the purely theatrical for a comedy of manners that portrayed faithfully the life of the day, Mrs. Mowatt anticipated Tom Robertson by twenty years and forecast with precision the modern school of comedy. She was, however, an oasis in a desert of commonplaceness, and the real value of her work was not perceived. There appeared no one to develop as she had begun, and the achievement that should have been an impetus and an inspiration to the American theatre passed unnoticed and was made impotent by indifference. The time for the American drama had not arrived. There was no public for it.

Until Dion Boucicault, Augustin Daly, and Bronson Howard began to make their influence felt, all that the seasons had to show in the way of local plays were the crude representations of New York life, the " Mose " plays of F. S. Cranfrau, scattered bits of Yankee and negro caricature, the boisterous farces and burlesques, the Dickens and other dramatisations of John Brougham, and the few farces of William E. Burton, of which " The Toodles " was the best. The leading influence in New York after the middle of the century, and until Augustin Daly firmly established himself as a producing manager, was the Wallack family. James W. Wallack, Sr., and after him his son, J. Lester Wallack, were active in the dramatic field from the fall of 1842, when the house at the corner of Broadway and Broome Street, which had been Brougham's Lyceum, was opened as Wallack's Theatre, until 1887, when Lester Wallack retired from active management.   During that period three theatres were known as Wallack's, one at the corner of Broadway and Broome Street, the second on Thirteenth Street, afterward the Star, which was opened in 1861, and the third on Thirtieth Street, which was opened in 1882.   Although not a manager of a New York theatre, constantly supplementing the influence of the Wallack father and son, and adding to the lustre of the Wallack name, was James W. Wallack, Jr., Lester Wallack's cousin.   He was born in London in 1818, and was brought to the United States as an infant.   His first appearance on the stage was made in Philadelphia in 1822, as Cora's child in " Pizarro." He acted in New York for the first time at the National Theatre in 1838.   He starred for many years, and in 1860 formed the Wallack-

Davenport combination, Wallack himself making a great impression as Fagin in "Oliver Twist," to the Bill Sykes of E. L. Davenport and the Nancy of Rose Eytinge. Mathias, in "The Bells," was also considered one of Wallack's best parts. He died in 1873.

John Lester Wallack was born in New York, on January 1, 1820, but was taken to England when he was very young, for his father had not at that time decided to stay in the United States. Lester Wallack fitted himself for the army and secured his commission. Then he made up his mind that the stage was the place for him, and quit soldiering almost before he had begun. The first record of his acting is in Dublin in 1842, when, under the name of John W. Lester, which he kept until 1861, he played Don Pedro in "Much Ado About Nothing." On September 27, 1847, Wallack made his American début at the New York Broadway Theatre, as Sir Charles Coldstream, in Dion Boucicault's adaptation, "Used Up." Lester was the stage-manager of Wallack's Theatre when it was opened in 1852, and on the first night played Tangent, in Morton's comedy, "The

JAMES W. WALLACK, JR.

Way to Get Married." When the Thirteenth Street house was opened in 1861, the name of James W. Wallack was down as manager and remained so until his death in 1864, but Lester had the full charge of the house, in token of which he for the first time was known by his own name of Lester Wallack.

As an actor Wallack was remarkable for his versatility and brilliancy. He was especially fine as a light comedian and in parts romantically melodramatic. As a manager he was liberal within narrow limitations, but he was neither original nor progressive. He also wrote eight plays, as follows: "The Three Guardsmen" (1849); "The Four Musketeers" (1849); "The Fortune of War" (1851); "Two to One, or the King's Visit" (1854); "First Impression" (1856); "The Veteran" (1859); "Central Park" (1861); "Rosedale" (1863).

Wallack's Theatre was from the beginning more distinguished for its high-class acting than for its devotion to original drama. From its greenroom went forth a noble array of actors. For his repertory Lester Wallack was content with the standard comedies as long as the public would stand them, and when the public revolted, he knew no other place than England to look for something novel. As Wallack's friend, Julian Magnus, wrote: " Perhaps the most marked fault of Lester Wallack's management, and one that more than all others contributed to his later failures, was his extreme devotion to English plays and English actors. He failed to recognise the gradually growing demand for American plays and players; and though, at long intervals, he gave an American author a chance, he was not fortunate in his selections, and did not seem to be much grieved at failure."

Dion Boucicault (1822–90) first came to the United States in 1853, and thereafter he was for years at a time intimately connected with the American stage. Many of his plays were produced in this country before they were given in London, and the best known of these were: " The Octoroon " (1859), " The Colleen Bawn " (1860), and " The Shaughran " (1874), in all of which Boucicault himself appeared; " The Long Strike " and " Led Astray," which were done by stock companies; and " The Jilt," a five-act comedy, writ-

DION BOUCICAULT.

ten for Louise Thorndyke-Boucicault and first played in 1885. Boucicault kept the American managers and actors busily employed for a good many years, and even now a stock company occasionally has the temerity to resurrect " The Colleen Bawn " or " The Shaughran ; " but, in the face of this evidence of longevity, it is doubtful if the Boucicault drama has really exerted the slightest permanent influence on the theatre either for good or for bad. Boucicault's Irish melodramas were flattering to an impressionable and emotional race, which honestly believed itself truthfully reflected in the bubbling good nature of Conn the Shaughran and Myles-na-Coppaleen, and in the carefully labelled virtues of Daddy O'Dowd. This race has been faithfully trying to live up to the part ever since. Boucicault was the creator of a peculiar type of stage Irishman, which never did and never will exist; and when, therefore, one recalls the monotonous series of these stage Irishmen, with which the theatre has been afflicted, all modelled after Boucicault's fancy sketch, he can scarcely be expected to wax particularly enthusiastic over Boucicault's influence on the drama.   Boucicault had his day, and let us be grateful that his day was yesterday.

The theatrical manager who usurped the place so long held by the Wallacks was John Augustin Daly (1838–99), who assumed the charge of his first playhouse in 1869, and who was firmly established in the van of all his competitors when Clara Morris made her New York début in the fall of 1870, as Anne Sylvester, in Daly's dramatisation of Wilkie Collins's "Man and Wife."   Daly had been a newspaper man before he turned his hand to play - writing.   His first effort in the dramatic line was "A Bachelor's Romance," which William E. Burton refused to produce.   In 1862, however, Daly scored a success with "Leah the Forsaken," which he adapted from Mosenthal's "Deborah," and in 1867 he secured still more popular vogue with his sensational melodrama, "Under the Gaslight."   That was practically the only original work which Daly ever did, and though for nearly thirty years he provided his company with plays, of which he usually claimed the authorship, they were adaptations from French and German sources.   In addition, he "arranged" all the Shakespearian plays and all the old comedies which his company acted.

It was an odd circumstance that the play which made Augustin Daly was " Under the Gaslight," a sensational melodrama, and that the play which he last produced was " The Great Ruby," a sensational melodrama. This was a coincidence, which might be construed as a suggestive commentary on Augustin Daly's life-work. Mr. Daly was a great manager, the greatest producing manager and the greatest stage-manager of his time. He became remarkably skilled in the regulating of theatrical effect, and, although a martinet, he certainly knew how to train actors so that their team-work, regardless of their individual abilities, was noteworthy. For years he was the acknowledged head of his profession, and although for several seasons before his death his influence had been diminishing, the cause was not so much that Daly was in his decline as that the American stage had made tremendous progress along the Daly lines, a condition for which Daly himself was chiefly responsible. Daly was many times a pioneer;

he refused to follow tamely the lead of the English theatre, and in breaking away he introduced the German farce and fathered the emotional drama of the French. With his company he invaded England itself, and even the Continent, and finally he "popularised" Shakespeare. He seemed to be, and he doubtless was, a manager with an ideal. That is to say, he was anxious to accomplish something better than the ordinary. But his motives were not of the highest, for he counted continually the profit to himself either in reputation or in cash. Nor was he a man of much natural fineness of nature, or of any great native refinement, culture, and taste. Consequently his appreciation of the genuinely artistic was meagre. His purpose to foster what he conceived to be the artistic in the drama constantly brought curious and paradoxical results, because his inherent instinct was prosaic and theatrical, and his trained judgment inartistic and material. To gratify his own idea of what was best in the drama, he was ruthless in his treatment of the text of great English plays, and so lavish with his pageantry in the staging of them, that many of his most ambitious productions were marvels of misconceived and misapplied effort.

Augustin Daly's influence, however, was vastly more enduring than that of Boucicault, for Daly did have some sort of an ideal, and that counted for something. Boucicault, on the contrary, never dreamed that there was such a thing as an ideal. The practical value of Daly's many years of hard work has been much overestimated, however. A large percentage of his time was given over to the production of German farce, which, after it had acquainted the public with the excellence of bright, snappy, and sparkling light comedy acting, had nothing more to give. Mr. Daly's Shakespearian productions kept, it is true, the name of Shakespeare on the stage, but it is doubtful if they were especially instrumental in cultivating a taste for the Shakespearian dramas. In fact, one might argue that they really did more harm than good by inculcating a false notion of what a stage representation of Shakespeare should be. Like the Wallacks, however, Mr. Daly was successful in developing a great many brilliant players, and in that circumstance was his chief glory.

He knew how to train actors, and there is immortality for him in the list that includes Clara Morris, Fanny Davenport, Ada Rehan, Mrs. G. H. Gilbert, John Drew, Maurice Barrymore, James E. Lewis, and Otis Skinner.

CHAPTER V.

URING the fifteen years between 1875 and 1890, the changes that took place in the American theatre and in the American drama were marvellous. It is true that they were greater in the mechanics of the stage and in the training of actors than they were in the perfection of play-writing; yet the American drama did make a certain advance during that period, and there came into being in that time all the dramatists who are now considered the leaders in this country. Many there were, too, who flourished ephemerally in that decade and a half, and who since then have become fading memories, — Benjamin E. Woolf, whose " The Mighty Dollar," with the Florences in the leading parts, was for years a great money-maker; the poet Joaquin Miller, now scarcely recalled as a dramatist, but whose " The Danites " was so successful that in 1880 it encouraged McKee Rankin to take to England the first complete American company to appear in that country; Bartley Campbell, whose melodramas hit the masses hard; Steele Mackaye, the apostle of Delsarte and the author of " Hazel Kirke " and " Paul Kauvar." In that period, also, the sentimental and naïve emotional drama as exemplified in " The Wife " and " The Charity Ball," by Henry DeMille and David Belasco had its day, while the curious phenomenon of the efficacy of caricature, displayed so fully in the entertainments of Charles H. Hoyt and Edward H. Harrigan, was a passing phase of interest.

The life-giving quality in plays like " The Mighty Dollar," " The Danites," and Bartley Campbell's " My Partner " was their really virile, though somewhat exaggerated, studies of American character and, in a rude way, of certain American conditions. Woolf in Bartwell Slote portrayed, with sufficient truthfulness to make the satire understood and the humour effective, a type of the American politician unfortunately common enough to be familiar. William H. Crane's Hannibal Rivers, in " The Senator," showed the same type of character somewhat more refined and a trifle more subtly treated. Miller in " The Danites " pictured a phase of Western life with which he was thoroughly acquainted, and the reality of his scenes made them comprehensible to those who knew nothing about them at first hand.   The same virtues were in evidence also in " My Partner," which, however, depended more on theatrical effect than it did on fidelity to its environment. These vitalising qualities in " The Danites " and " My Partner " have since been utilised with higher dramatic effect by Augustus Thomas in " In Mizzoura " and " Arizona." Faulty construction, obvious development, and conventional theatrical devices were found in abundance in these plays by Woolf, Miller, and Campbell, but they were considerably offset by the brilliant acting of Mr. and Mrs. William J. Florence, of Mr. and Mrs. McKee Rankin, and of Louis Aldrich and Charles T. Parsloe, Jr.

BARTLEY CAMPBELL

Bartley Campbell (1842–88), though only a deviser of sensational melodrama, was in some respects a remarkable man. He apparently barely missed being a genius, thereby becoming that pathetic thing, known as brilliantly erratic. Although he had far more original ability than the men about him who succeeded, Campbell made a failure of everything he tried, except the writing of wild melodramas, and he died abject and poor, under the most tragic circumstances. He was born in Pittsburg, Pennsylvania, and his first attempt at play-writing was in 1871, when his " Through Fire " was produced. His other plays were: 1872, " Peril " and " Life at Long Branch;" 1873, " Fate," " Risks," and " The Virginian;" 1874, " Gran Uale;" 1875, " On the Rhine " and " The Big Bonanza," adapted from the German comedy " Ultimo;" 1876, " A Hero in Rags," " How Women Love," which was afterward called " The Heart of the Sierras," and then reconstructed and named " The Vigilantes;" 1878, " Clio;" 1879, " Fairfax " and " My Partner;" 1880, " The Galley Slave " and " My Geraldine;" 1882, " The White Slave " and " Friend and Foe;" 1884, " Siberia " and " Separation;" 1885, " Paquita." " Fate " was produced at the Olympic, London, by Carlotta Leclercq in 1884. "The Galley Slave" was done in Hull, England, in 1880, and in London in 1886. "Siberia" was played in London in 1887.

STEELE MACKAYE'S "HAZEL KIRKE"

Steele Mackaye's "Hazel Kirke" for a long time — perhaps it does still — held the "long run" record in this country, and for that reason the curious way in which the play grew into popular favour is interesting. Steele Mackaye became a New York manager in the spring of 1879, when he opened the Madison Square Theatre on the site that had been occupied by Augustin Daly's Fifth Avenue Theatre, which had burned on January 1, 1873. When Mackaye took the place it was known as Minnie Cummings's Drawing-Room Theatre, and burlesques were given there by a company that included Vernona Jarbeau and Louise Beaudet. Mackaye spent the entire fall and most of the winter in remodelling the place and in installing the famous double stage, his own idea, which, however, never proved of much practical use. He engaged a company, of which Eben Plympton,

C. W. Couldock, Rose Coghlan, Ada Gilman, B. T. Ringgold, and Effie Ellsler were the principal members, and Daniel Frohman the business manager. Inasmuch as the theatre was not ready for occupancy, these actors were sent on the road as the Madison Square Theatre Company, but no one had ever heard of any such theatre, so the name did not count for anything. The company opened at Low's Opera House, Providence, Rhode Island, on October 27, 1879, with a four-act comedy drama by Mackaye, called " An Iron Will," and the business was not large enough to pay the travelling expenses. " Hazel Kirke " was a slightly altered version of " An Iron Will." It was produced in New York at the opening of the rebuilt Madison Square Theatre on February 4, 1880, with Effie Ellsler as Hazel Kirke, C. W. Couldock as Dunstan Kirke, and Eben Plympton as Lord Travers. The plan was to run it six weeks, but the critics condemned it on the opening night and business declined rapidly. So during the first week " Masks and Faces," with Rose Coghlan as Peg Woffington, was put into rehearsal. Then, for some unaccountable reason, " Hazel Kirke " took a sudden turn. The size of the audiences increased, and in a short time it was a case of crowded houses at all performances. The run of " Hazel Kirke " continued until May 31, 1881, when it was withdrawn after its four hundred and eighty-sixth consecutive performance, during which time Rose Coghlan had drawn eight thousand dollars in salary as a member of the company, without having made a single public appearance. During the run of " Hazel Kirke " Georgia Cayvan made her New York début on November 9, 1880, as Dolly Dutton, succeeding Gabriel DuSauld, who created the part; and the Hazel Kirkes after Effie Ellsler were Jeffreys Lewis, Jean Burnside, Carrie Wyatt, Carrie Turner, Bijou Heron (Mrs. Henry Miller), Maud Osborn (Mrs. Gustav Frohman), and Annie Russell. Henry Miller acted Travers on the road, as did Edwin Arden, Henry Lee, Charles B. Welles, and J. G. Grahame.

EDWARD HARRIGAN

Edward Harrigan and Charles H. Hoyt were the direct successors of negro minstrelsy and the legitimate forerunners of " polite vaudeville."   Harrigan, who was born in New York on October 26, 1845, and made his first appearance on the stage in San Francisco in 1867, began by playing Irish characters in the old-time variety shows.   Forming in 1871 a partnership with Tony Hart, and the team requiring a sketch, Harrigan forthwith wrote one.   From that careless start developed the peculiar Harrigan entertainment, the first one of which was " The Mulligan Guards," done with remarkable success at the Theatre Comique, New York, in 1878.   For ten years after that the Harrigan shows were produced on an average of two a season, and they continued almost invariably popular until the especial phase of New York life that they depicted became a thing of the past, and, therefore, the portrayal of it on the stage ceased longer to interest.   Harrigan's best known works were: " The Mulligan Guards' Ball" and " The Mulligan Guards' Chowder Party," in 1879; " The Major," in 1881; " Squatter Sovereignty," " Mordecai Lyons " (his first failure), and " McSorley's Flirtation," in 1882; " The Muddy Day " and " Cordelia's Aspirations," in 1883; " Dan's

Tribulations," in 1884; "Old Lavender," in 1885; "The Leather Patch" and "The Reagans," in 1886; "McNooney's Visit" (afterward "4-11-44") and "Pete," in 1887; "Waddy Googan" and "Reilly and the 400," in 1888.

Critical comment on the Harrigan shows is quite impossible. It is true that William Dean Howells once discovered Mr. Harrigan and labelled him with some high-sounding title and deduced from his work many edifying conclusions; but I am afraid that Mr. Howells was more interested in hatching a theory than he was in giving a thoroughly trustworthy estimate of the value of Mr. Harrigan's amusements. I am equally sure that no one was so surprised to learn how great he was as Mr. Harrigan himself. The Harrigan shows were not developed plays with a connected dramatic interest. They were a collection of detached episodes, roughly united by the circumstance that the same characters appeared in all of them. These episodes were bits of typical low life in New York, reproduced with approximate truthfulness, though naturally the low comedy element was violently emphasised.   The humour was noisy, coarse, and vulgar, but that was the worst that could be said of it.   It was never indecent nor suggestive.   Songs and dancing, rowing and fighting were utilised to eke out the places where the interest threatened to collapse.

As is always the case in entertainments of the Harrigan sort, the really strong element that they possessed was found in the characters.   In the Harrigan product, the characters were not so much the invention of Harrigan himself as they were of the capable character actors with whom he surrounded himself. Harrigan indicated the type that he wanted, and the players built up the character.   Thus the jovial, unctuous, and unexaggerated Irishman of Harrigan, the richly brogued and irresistibly funny Irishwoman of Mrs. Annie Yeamans, and the bumptious negro of John Wild were the real backbone and substance of all the Harrigan pieces.   Without them, William Dean Howells notwithstanding,   there would have been nothing left but void and incomprehensible nonsense.

CHARLES H. HOYT

From the time that Charles H. Hoyt (1860–1900) made his first success, in 1884, with " A Bunch of Keys," in which Willie Edouin and Alice Atherton appeared for several years, until his death, there was not a theatrical season passed in this country without at least one, and usually more than one, of the Hoyt pieces being played for the full number of weeks with satisfactory profit. Like Harrigan, Hoyt never wrote a real play, unless, by stretching a point, " A Midnight Bell " and " A Texas Steer," his two best works, be brought into the farce category. The characteristically Hoytian piece was a formless thing made up of lively antics by nimble entertainers, songs and dances strung together on a skeleton plot, humour that was chiefly acrobatic and noisy, and wit that was brought in from the street through the stage door. Yet these " farce-comedies " amused their tens of thousands, and persons, who had scarcely even heard of Shakespeare, knew by heart the conceits and the quibbles of " A Rag Baby," " A Parlour Match," " A Brass Monkey," " A Trip to Chinatown," " A Temperance

Town," " A Milk-White Flag," and " A Black Sheep."

With the exception of " A Midnight Bell," " A Texas Steer," and " A Temperance Town," Hoyt's pieces were more inconsequential than Harrigan's; but Hoyt had a faculty of placing on the stage more widely diversified types of character than did Harrigan, and Hoyt's characters, as momentary and unanalysed impressions, were lifelike and effective caricatures. Thus his Old Sport, as done by Frank Daniels in " A Rag Baby," was a worthy low comedy study, while his Texas Congressman, played by Tim Murphy in " A Texas Steer," was on a decidedly higher plane and revealed something very close to character development.   Most of Hoyt's work, however, never arose above the mother-in-law level of wit and humour or the Weary Waggles style of character delineation. His immense vogue was due much more to the way in which his pieces were presented than it was to the pieces themselves.   He hired attractive women and versatile men, and he trained them to sputter and crackle like a bunch of Fourth of July firecrackers under a barrel.   His actors were so physically indefatigable that they compelled attention, and they raised such a bustle of bogus excitement that the customary intelligence of the vast majority of spectators was lost in the shuffle, and they were fooled into believing that they were having a grand, good time.

WILLIAM YOUNG

Aside from George Henry Boker (1823–90), who joined with the art of verse-making that of diplomacy, whose tragedy " Calaynos " was played by E. L. Davenport, and whose " Francesca da Rimini " was successfully given by Lawrence Barrett and Otis Skinner, one of the very few American dramatists to win the slightest serious or lasting consideration for his drama in verse has been William Young, whose latest and probably most widely known achievement was the dramatisation (in prose) of General Lew Wallace's novel, " Ben Hur." Mr. Young's " Pendragon," a dramatic rendering of the pith of the Arthurian legends, first brought him into general notice. It was given an elaborate stage production by Lawrence Barrett in 1881, and was received with remarkable favour. The critics of the country praised it with surprising unanimity and warmth ; and though a tragedy and in verse, — and so in two respects sadly handicapped from the box-office point of view, — it appealed also with notable success to the popular fancy.

In 1883 " The Rajah," a comedy in prose, was presented by the Madison Square Theatre Company. The critics, who, in the case of " Pendragon," had treated the dramatist with exceptional favour, not only condemned " The Rajah " as a work of art, but consigned it summarily to oblivion. However, the play against which this crushing verdict was pronounced, ran for two hundred and fifty nights at the Madison Square, was for several seasons after that a leading attraction on the road, and still later was successfully presented in Australia.

In his next important venture Mr. Young returned to verse. In 1889, he completed " Ganelon," a semi-historic, romantic tragedy, calling for costly scenic effects and archæological appointments ; and again he found a patron in Lawrence Barrett. The play was produced with great splendour and was signally success-ful, Mr. Barrett managing the enterprise and appearing in the title part. In the middle of the season, however, its career was interrupted by Mr. Barrett's illness, from which he never fully recovered. Among Mr. Young's other contributions to dramatic literature, a free adaptation, in verse, of Jules Barbier's " Jeanne d'Arc" is worthy of mention. This was given in sumptuous style at the Fifth Avenue Theatre, New York, in 1891, the production rivalling in lavishness of scenic display Bernhardt's famous presentation of the piece at the Porte St. Martin.

By birth Mr. Young is a Westerner. He was graduated from an Illinois college and followed this by studying law. But, before he had been admitted to the bar, he had seen his first play, " Jonquil," produced at Booth's Theatre, and abandoning the law, he spent some time familiarising himself with the stage as an actor, after which he studied stage-craft abroad with the best masters of the art that he could find.

BRONSON HOWARD

Augustin Daly was never interested in American plays, except such as he made himself from the ground plan of the German farce and the French connubial drama.   Yet Augustin Daly was responsible for the first success of the man, who, probably more than any other, is entitled to rank as the leading American dramatist.   Bronson Howard became notorious through the popularity of his frivolous and vulgar farce, "Saratoga," which was produced by Daly in the early seventies; but Mr. Howard's reputation was solidly established by some half dozen later dramas that ranged from light comedy to vigorous melodrama.   These six plays were: "Old Love Letters," "The Banker's Daughter," "Young Mrs. Winthrop," "The Henrietta," "Shenandoah," and "Aristocracy."   In all, however, Mr. Howard has been responsible for sixteen plays, produced as follows:

"Fantine" (1862); taken from Victor Hugo's "Les Miserables" and produced in Detroit, where it ran for a week.

"Saratoga" (1870); produced by Augustin Daly at the Fifth Avenue Theatre, New York, where it was given one hundred and eight times.   It was also acted in London by Charles Wyndham, under the title, "Brighton."

"Diamonds" (1872); also produced at the

Fifth Avenue Theatre, where it was played for fifty-six nights.

"Moorcroft, or the Double Wedding" (1874); a failure, at the Fifth Avenue Theatre. It dealt with the subject of slavery.

"Hurricanes" and "Old Love Letters" (1878); produced the same night at the Park Theatre, New York. "Hurricanes" was a sort of forerunner of the Charles H. Hoyt "farce-comedies."

"The Banker's Daughter" (1878); produced at the Union Square Theatre, New York. It was tried originally in Chicago in 1873, under the title, "Lillian's First Love," but was entirely rewritten for the New York production. It was acted in London in 1879 as "The Old Love and the New."

"Wives" (1879); adaptation from Molière, produced at Daly's Theatre.

"Baron Rudolph" (1880); afterward rewritten with the aid of David Belasco and presented by George S. Knight, but not successfully.

"Young Mrs. Winthrop" (1882); produced at the Madison Square Theatre, New York, where it ran the whole season.

" One of Our Girls " (1885); produced at the Lyceum Theatre, New York, with Helen Dauvray in the leading part.

" Met by Chance " (1887); written for Helen Dauvray, and produced at the Lyceum Theatre. It was a complete failure, and never was acted but once.

" The Henrietta " (1887); produced at the Union Square Theatre, New York, with Stuart Robson and William H. Crane in the leading parts.

" Shenandoah " (1888); produced at the Boston Museum, revised and presented at the Star Theatre, New York, afterward transferred to Proctor's Theatre, where it ran the entire season of 1889–90.

" Aristocracy " (1892); produced at Palmer's Theatre, New York.

" Peter Stuyvesant " (1899); written in collaboration with Brander Matthews and produced in Providence, Rhode Island, with William H. Crane in the title part. It was a quick failure.

Apart from this chronicle of plays, there is very little of a biographical nature to tell regarding Bronson Howard. He was born in Detroit, Michigan, on October 7, 1842. His father, Charles Howard, who was Mayor of Detroit in 1849, was a member of the old Oswego shipping firm of Alvin, Bronson & Company, and it was after one of the senior partners that Bronson Howard was named. Mr. Howard expected to enter Yale so as to be graduated with the class of 1865, but his eyesight failed, and he went into newspaper work instead. In 1867 he became connected with the New York *Evening Gazette*, and later with the *Evening Mail*, the *Tribune*, and the *Evening Post*. In 1875 he went to England, and for several months was a contributor to the *Pall Mall Gazette*. He represented that paper and the *Detroit Free Press* at the Philadelphia Centennial in 1876. Visiting England again in 1879, he married there, in 1880, the sister of Charles Wyndham, the English actor.

As a dramatist, Mr. Howard was at his best in light comedy, where his talent for writing witty and at the same time dramatically effect-ive dialogue, and his strong grasp of situa-tions, were displayed at their best. He was at his worst in his serious dramas, although many of them were exceedingly successful with the public.   In his serious works his extremely conventional views of life, his shallow and ordinary motives, and his inherent snobbishness were baldly uncovered. Moreover, in writing dialogue for these plays, he lost largely the easy and graceful style found in his lighter work, and was prone to mount the high horse of stilted elegance.   In such plays as " The Banker's Daughter" and " Aristocracy," all of Mr. Howard's characters resided in residences, and they invited one another to be seated in drawing-rooms, from which they retired for a night's rest.   In no one work did Mr. Howard declare the best that was in him so effectually as in " Old Love Letters," a one-act comedietta, which bordered on the sentimental but never quite emerged into it, which was exquisite in feeling, delicate in pathos, spontaneous and delightful in the 'fine sensibility of its humour, and genuine in its sincerity.   To see this playlet, with all its subtilties and suggestions, revealed by the insinuating and authoritative art of Agnes Booth, was indeed a theatrical experience, rich, full, and complete.

Mr. Howard's first play of the " intense " school was " The Banker's Daughter," a strong and worthy acting drama, but displaying as part of the very fibre of its theme and characters, and in the manner both theme and characters were treated, that snobbishness which spoiled all of Mr. Howard's more ambitious efforts. The detailing of the plot and the description of the "high life" of the play's personages are enough to show what is meant. Lilian, the daughter of a wealthy New York banker, is in love with an artist, Harold Routledge. The drama opens just after she has quarrelled with him and broken their engagement. At her father's earnest solicitation, she marries John Strebelow, a wealthy man of noble and honourable nature. She respects her husband, idolises her daughter, and is, in fact, comfortably happy until she encounters her former lover in Paris. They have a private meeting, and quickly discover that they were tricked and deceived by Lilian's father, who desired the marriage with Strebelow in order to save his own credit. However, after declaring their unchanged affection for each other, the couple separate, resolved never to meet again.

But their talk has been overheard by Count

Carojac, a rejected suitor of Lilian, who forces Harold to a duel and kills him. Just as the fatal thrust is given, Strebelow and Lilian appear on the scene, and her horror at the conflict, and grief at the death, cause her to betray her feelings for the murdered man. An explanation between her and her husband follows, with the result, that while he believes fully in her truth and honour, he decides that a separation is necessary. So they part, she taking the child with her, and they do not meet again for seven years, when a reconciliation and reunion is happily effected by the good offices of the daughter.

"Young Mrs. Winthrop" was open to many of the objections urged against "The Banker's Daughter." It was of much the same style and character, though rather more original, simple, and ingenious. The dialogue, too, was fresher and brighter, and the characters were better assorted and more effective. It contained much that was really pathetic, while a serious and elevated tone pervaded the entire drama. The story is that of a husband and wife whose little differences have grown into grave misunderstandings that have alienated their affections completely. The husband forsakes his home more and more for his business and his club; and the wife, neglected and craving companionship, rushes headlong into the maelstrom of fashionable society. The mother of the husband points out to him the result of such a condition, and he resolves to acknowledge his faults and to win back his wife's love. She has discovered, however, that her husband has been corresponding with a woman of whom he has openly disapproved. The wife comes to the conclusion that her husband has been false to her. This opinion is strengthened by the gossip of one of her friends. She therefore repels his advances, and, in defiance of his authority, goes to a ball, where she hears other things derogatory to her husband. Returning home, she finds her child stricken with a sudden illness. Her husband again seeks a reconciliation, but she repulses him, and, when the child dies, turns from him with bitterness and hatred. The couple come to the conclusion that they can live together no longer, and seek the family lawyer to arrange the terms of the separation. The lawyer, however, thinks otherwise, and by calling up old memories and referring to the dead child, he quickens the love that seems dead, and husband and wife are reunited.

Mr. Howard's best work, however, was still to come, and it proved to be " The Henrietta," perhaps, all things considered, the best light comedy that the American theatre has produced. " The Henrietta " was acted for the first time in the fall of 1887, after Mr. Howard had experienced the worst failure of his career, with " Met by Chance," written to order for Helen Dauvray.

" The play," said Mr. Howard, in a reference to this mournful circumstance, " was entirely out of my line, and the character did not suit Miss Dauvray. The critics tore the piece all to bits. Some of them hinted that I had gone into a mental decline. After reading their strictures in the morning papers, I began to think I had committed some criminal offence. I was mad all the way through. At the time I was under contract to Robson and Crane to write ' The Henrietta,' and I took the train for Washington, where they were playing an engagement. I thought they had probably lost faith in my ability to write plays. They greeted

STUART ROBSON

As Bertie in "The Henrietta."

me very cordially, and the first allusion to the failure of 'Met by Chance' set them grinning in a most exasperating manner. Finally I couldn't stand their seeming delight in my recent discomfiture, and told them pointblank that I didn't consider the failure of my piece a subject of unseemly mirth.

"'No,' said Robson, 'but we are tickled to death over it.'

"'You see,' added Crane, 'we knew that you had never had an out-and-out failure. We knew, too, that it was bound to come sooner or later, and we didn't want it to strike us. That's why we're so hilarious over the failure of "Met by Chance."'

"This extraordinary explanation caused me to join in the laugh. I returned to New York, and worked on 'The Henrietta' as I had never worked before in the whole course of my life. I set my teeth with the determination to show the New York critics that I was not suffering from softening of the brain, and was capable of turning out just as good a play as I had ever written before."

"The Henrietta" is a finished product, logical in construction, and swift and apt in dialogue.   Headed continually toward farce, it is as continually saved from immersion into the essential artificiality of farce by the downright strength and humanity of its characters and the fine legitimacy of its studies of life. " The Henrietta " is, moreover, thoroughly American. It sets forth with consistency and fidelity the paradoxical seriousness and humour of the American man — particularly the American business man. Mr. Howard not only makes plain the racking nervous tension of Wall Street speculation, but he notes with equal vividness the far subtler element of " sport," which makes so fascinating to many this huge game of finance and guesswork. The dramatist's method is as straightforward as it is effective. In contrast with the gloomy, material, and sordid background suggested by the nerve-racked and desperate Wall Street gambler, he places the light, frivolous, and thoroughly inconsequential Bertie, the meekest and the most abject of all lambs. Accompanying the ludicrous predicaments into which this gentle character strays is the development of the highly dramatic plot, in which " Old Nick," the Napoleon of the " Street," is so vitally concerned. Finally, with both art and technique, these two contrasting features of the play are brought into absolute unison for the final climax, and, at length, choicest morsel of all, Bertie the lamb, the butt of everybody's ridicule, becomes, without an illogical step or the least reversal of character, the essential pivot on which the action hinges, the one person who is complete master of the situation, financially and otherwise.

Now that William Gillette has shown, by his original "Secret Service," the dramatic possibilities in the war play, "Shenandoah" has become both old-fashioned and conventional. Yet, except for Mr. Gillette's "Held by the Enemy," it was the pioneer among the higher class of war dramas; and its success was not only the inspirer of "Secret Service," but also of David Belasco's "The Heart of Maryland," Franklin Fyles's "The Girl I Left Behind Me," James A. Herne's "Griffith Davenport," and to some degree of that fine military melodrama, Augustus Thomas's "Arizona." "Shenandoah" was an out-and-out melodrama, and in it action and theatrical effect were of paramount importance.

Character counted for nothing at all. Written around the schoolboy's favourite poem, "Sheridan's Ride,"—now said to commemorate a fictitious incident,—the play was staged with the superlative of scenic splendour, and both the trappings and to a mild extent the horrors of war were utilised to give colour and movement on the stage. It was, in fact, the details in the embellishment of the piece that made the most lasting impression, and the representation of signalling by torches, which was managed with exceptional illusion, was vividly remembered after the recollection of plot and characters became dim.

Mr. Howard's last play to meet with success was " Aristocracy," which displayed in the plainest fashion the temperamental faults that had been perceived to some extent in " The Banker's Daughter" and " Young Mrs. Winthrop." In " Aristocracy " the dramatist indulged in the gentle sport of letting the eagle scream, and his main argument was that all the good men and women were either dead, poor, or of obscure parentage. Consideration of this theory apparently aroused Mr. Howard's temper to most undignified asperity, and he proclaimed with acridity that all " American aristocrats," those with *Mayflower* ancestors and such like, were persons with whom decent folks would better have as little to do as possible, and that all real English aristocrats were persons whom one ought not to touch with a ten-foot pole. In fact, his only truly respectable individual (native or foreign) in the United States was a self-made millionaire. All the others were downright and hopeless cads. Mr. Howard's telling of his tale inclined toward the lurid, though it was cleverly worked out even when it was improbable.

It is, indeed, a pity that a dramatist with Mr. Howard's unquestioned natural and cultivated gifts and undoubted excellencies as a constructor of plays, as a delineator of character, and as a writer of dialogue, should not have combined with these a truer thought, a more steadfast ideal, and a greater appreciation of really vital psychological and sociological problems. It is true that a play is neither an essay nor a thesis; but it is equally true that every superior play must declare conditions that might well inspire an essay or a thesis; and it is the dramatist's definiteness of opinion regarding those underlying conditions and his just estimate of them that gives character and force and conviction to his work. Mr. Howard had all the needful embellishments for the pursuit of the profession of playwriting, but character, force, and conviction he assuredly lacked.

CHAPTER VI.

COMING to the stage of the present moment, four American dramatists are found to have secured positions, none of them on the heights of Parnassus, but all, as William Warren said of himself, comfortably situated in sheltered niches on the side of the mountain. These are William Gillette, who, of the four, is the most solid in his technical equipment and the most certain regarding the effects that he secures in his work; James A. Herne, who was (for he is the only one of the four that is dead) the most original in his conceptions and the most daring in his execution of them, who was the deepest thinker, the keenest analyser, and the most artistically natured; Clyde Fitch, who is both the most prolific and the most disappointing, but who is excelled by none of them in ability to place modern social amenities on the stage with artistic realism; and Augustus Thomas, who is the least to be depended upon and who has done both the best and the worst work of the quartette.

Gillette and Herne were accustomed to write plays for their own acting, and that fact definitely determined the character of their dramas. Thus Gillette, an actor of striking repose and marvellous suggestion, writing plays for his own use, developed personages that he could act most effectively, and set them in dramatic pieces that called for the exercise of the histrionic qualities that he could best provide. His finest plays are melodramas of an extremely subtle nature, wherein the dramatic interest is intense but always subdued, and wherein not violence but constant mental alertness and nervous energy are the most essential factors. Mr. Herne was a character actor of remarkable art, and in the depicting of certain types of rural character, and in the portraying of certain quiet though forceful qualities of emotion, not to be excelled. In accord with his own especial capacity, Mr. Herne's most successful plays were of the rural type, slightly melodramatic in tone, with, nevertheless, so rich a vein of humanity in their composition that the theatric quality was readily ignored in the satisfactory appreciation of their exceptional comedy.

WILLIAM GILLETTE

Although William Gillette is the author and the adapter of more than a dozen plays, — " The Professor," " The Private Secretary," " Esmeralda," " A Legal Wreck," " Held by the Enemy," " Because She Loved Him So," " Settled Out of Court," " Too Much Johnson," " Mr. Wilkinson's Widows," " All the Comforts of Home," " Clarice Morland," " Secret Service," and " Sherlock Holmes," — it is on three plays only that his reputation is established. These are " Held by the Enemy," " Secret Service," and " Sherlock Holmes," the trio forming an unusually interesting series. " Held by the Enemy " (1886) was plain melodrama without frills, but it was, even at that, a strong and interesting play, the flavour of which has not yet departed, in spite of the fact that its most striking incidents and its most novel situations have been borrowed right and left to decorate and enliven the works of less inventive and ingenious playwrights.

"Secret Service" (1895) declared the full vigour of Mr. Gillette's dramatic talent. It was a wonderfully vivid, intense, and compelling melodrama, in which the theatrical elements of suspense and sustained interest, of contrast and sympathetic appeal, were utilised in a thoroughly masterly manner. When Mr. Gillette himself appeared in the play, the cause of the drama's wonderful effectiveness and acting perfection seemed to lie in the strength and the intensity of Mr. Gillette's acting. Later, however, I saw a young actor, entirely different from Mr. Gillette in his methods, in Mr. Gillette's part. He was also surrounded by a distinctly inferior company. Yet he, too, secured in the play the tribute of eager attention and complete absorption that were always in evidence when Mr. Gillette played Captain Thorn. There is but one explanation of these parallel instances, — the play itself is compelling, wholly apart from the manner in which it is acted.

In both "Secret Service" and "Sherlock Holmes" (1899), action is the thing of main

WILLIAM GILLETTE

importance. I doubt if in either one of them there is dialogue enough to furnish three acts of an average four-act play. The plots are developed with a directness and a certainty that cannot be escaped. There are no explanations, and there are no diversions. Everything is placed before one through the mediumship of action, always vivid, interesting, and straight to the point. Minutes sometimes pass without a word being spoken on the stage, yet every move claims the undivided attention. The suspense engendered is carried almost to the unbearable point at the instant that it is adroitly broken by an intervening episode.

"Secret Service" was distinctly an honest play; "Sherlock Holmes" was frank and shameless buncombe. However, by openly acknowledging the utter impossibility of his dramatic incidents, and by cheerfully proclaiming that he was deliberately ladling out rank sensationalism, Mr. Gillette scored his most masterly point. He thereby disarmed all criticism, made quick friends with his audience, and brought about a mental condition that was divested of all antagonism and was eager and impressionable. The highest achievement of Mr. Gillette's art was reached when he succeeded in getting Conan Doyle's conception of Sherlock Holmes on the stage without robbing the character of a single one of its subtle charms or reducing it to an uninteresting condition of commonplace obviousness. Indeed, if anything, Mr. Gillette, by vivifying Holmes's personality, made him even more alluring than he was in the book; and at the same time the dramatist retained in full Holmes's imaginative appeal, and added, without spoiling the effect, a faint touch of heart interest and sentiment, touching the part with the shadow of pathos. By his complete and unique realisation of this fantastic, imaginative, and at the same time potently human conception, by his accurate transferral of the impossible, but none the less convincing, detective, from the intangible atmosphere of the book to the definite materialism of the stage, Mr. Gillette earned the reward of unqualified commendation. It was more than mere trickery; it was positive achievement.

JAMES A. HERNE

As a playwright, James A. Herne had one serious blemish that marred to some extent all his work and did its worst in preventing Mr. Herne's best play from becoming even a partial popular success. Mr. Herne lacked tenacity and logic. He had the stage-manager's appreciation of the dramatic value of a single incident or climax, and occasionally, as in the jarring storm scene in "Shore Acres" (1892), this appreciation led him into inharmonious effects; but Mr. Herne did not appreciate the value of accumulative energy. He did not develop his plays along one direct and determined line, and he did not stick to his theme with relentless persistency. It sometimes seemed as if he actually failed to grasp his work as a unit. It got away from him at times. One could imagine that he had begun to write his play with no very definite idea of what the conclusion of the matter would be or even where the middle would find him; he seemed content to let his plot meander along in a haphazard way wherever it chose to go, diving here and there into the byways and the hedges, unrestricted by the guiding and restraining thought that sees both the beginning and the end. The result was, of course, a loss of proportion and a haziness of construction that puzzled, bewildered, and, with " Griffith Davenport" (1899), literally ruined one of the loftiest conceived dramas that the American theatre has ever known.

It may perhaps seem contradictory that, with his laxness in other respects, Mr. Herne kept his characters consistently toeing the mark. Yet such was the fact. Mr. Herne possessed a keen insight into motive, and, no matter how straggling his construction might be, or how many loose ends his action might reveal, his characters rarely went in opposition to understood motive and settled environment. Mr. Herne placed his greatest stress and his chief reliance on character. This may seem a surprising statement to those who have been accustomed to much talking about Mr. Herne's realism, and who have failed to perceive that this realism was, after all, only the appropriate frame for Mr. Herne's characters. Atmosphere, for which Mr. Herne sought so persistently and which he obtained with such surety,

JAMES A. HERNE

As Griffith Davenport

was a necessity, because it instantly put one in touch with the personages of his plays. It was an important adjunct to Mr. Herne's supreme essential, the exposition of character.

CLYDE FITCH

Clyde Fitch is commonly accounted the leading dramatist at present writing for the American stage, but unless sheer muscle be taken as the chief qualification of a great playwright, it is doubtful if Mr. Fitch, being measured by any adequate standard of dramatic art, can be permitted to remain unprotested in the place that persistent reiteration of his name in the ears of the public has given him. If rating as a dramatist were parcelled out according to the number of plays to which one has attached his name, then Mr. Fitch would undoubtedly be entitled to first place among moderns; but, even at that, he would still be far behind the record of that zealous labourer in theatrical vineyards, Dion Boucicault, who was credited with the extraordinary number of four hundred original works and adaptations. With invention equal to that of the Yankee farmer bent on saving himself work, and with a productive capacity rivalled only by an incubator full of eggs, Boucicault averaged throughout his hard-working career about ten plays a year, though he was obliged to search zealously the foreign fields for material in order to attain that astounding result. Fitch has never yet written ten plays in a single year, but he has been abroad for material ; and, more than that, he has further proved himself Boucicault's ardent follower by utilising in at least one of his plays the same dramatic skeleton that Boucicault used in one of his. Such as desire to verify this statement may do so by comparing Mr. Fitch's " Captain Jinks of the Horse Marines " with Mr. Boucicault's " Grimaldi, or the Life of an Actress."

Clyde Fitch was born in Elmira, New York, on May 2, 1865, and was graduated from Amherst in 1886. His first play was " Beau Brummel," which Richard Mansfield produced at the Madison Square Theatre, New York, in 1890. This immediately became very popular and has remained in Mr. Mansfield's repertory ever since. The same year came two one-act plays, " Betty's Finish," which was brought out at the Boston Museum, and " Frédéric Lemaître," in which Henry Miller made one of his earliest and most pronounced successes. From that time on, Mr. Fitch's original plays and adaptations followed in rapid order. They may be summarised as follows:

"A Modern Match," produced in Minneapolis in 1891, and afterward acted in Ireland by Mr. and Mrs. Kendal, under the title of "Marriage."

"Pamela's Prodigy," produced in London in 1891 by Mrs. John Wood.

"The Masked Ball," from the French, produced by John Drew in 1892, giving Maude Adams a chance to make her first decided impression.

"A Shattered Idol," from Balzac's "Père Goriot," produced in 1893.

"An American Duchess," from the French of Henri Lavedan, produced in 1893.

"The Social Swim," produced by Marie Wainwright in 1893.

"Mr. Grundy, Jr.," from the French, produced in 1894.

"His Grace de Grammont," produced by Otis Skinner in 1894.

" April Weather," produced by Sol Smith Russell.

" Mistress Betty," produced by Modjeska in 1895.

" Gossip," adaptation done in collaboration with Leo Ditrichstein, and produced in 1895.

" Bohemia," from the French " La Vie de Bohème," by Henri Murger and Theodore Barrière, produced in 1896.

" The Liar," from the French of Bisson, produced in 1896.

" Nathan Hale," produced by Nat C. Goodwin and Maxine Elliott in 1898.

" The Moth and the Flame," rewritten from an earlier play called " The Harvest," and produced in 1898, afterward used as a starring vehicle by Effie Shannon and Herbert Kelcey.

" The Head of the Family," from the German, produced by William H. Crane in 1898.

" The Cowboy and the Lady," produced by Nat C. Goodwin and Maxine Elliott in 1899.

" Barbara Frietchie," produced by Julia Marlowe in 1899.

" Sapho," from the novel of Alphonse Daudet, produced by Olga Nethersole in 1900.

ETHEL BARRYMORE
As Madame Trentoni in "Captain Jinks of the Horse Marines"

" Captain Jinks of the Horse Marines," produced by Ethel Barrymore in 1901.

" The Climbers," produced by Amelia Bingham in 1901.

" Lovers' Lane," produced in 1901.

" The Marriage Game," adapted from the French, produced by Sadie Martinot in 1901.

" The Way of the World," produced by Elsie De Wolfe in 1901.

" The Last of the Dandies," produced by Beerbohm Tree in 1901.

" The Girl and the Judge," produced by Annie Russell in 1901.

The best of these recent plays and a very fair example of Mr. Fitch's capabilities was " The Climbers," the merits of which fairly balanced its obvious and rather exasperating blemishes. In accordance with his custom, Mr. Fitch started out very well; and by introducing his leading women characters immediately on their return from the funeral of the husband of one of them and the father of several others, the dramatist secured the novel, even startling, and to some, possibly, shocking effect, that he so dearly loves. It was Mr. Fitch's exceeding adroitness in presenting this cynical situation that saved it from positive condemnation on the score of bad taste. He was clever enough to turn it into an occasion for the exposition of character, shrewdly painting on this sombre background the shallow worldliness of the just widowed Mrs. Hunter; the equal worldliness, though a trifle modified by a grain of humour, of the daughter Cora, not yet "out"; the womanliness and the brave independence of the other two daughters, Blanche and Jessie; and finally the rich sympathy and the fine understanding of Miss Hunter, the maiden aunt. So neatly did the dramatist blend background into picture, that the background, with its brutal fling at death and mock at sorrow, was in a measure forgotten, and the act — with its frivolous women bartering, almost over the coffin, for the fine gowns that were now useless to the mourners, with its merciless uncovering of petty vanities, of snobbishness in its myriad forms, of rampant and degrading materialism — became a splendid specimen of satirical comedy. The covert sneer was on the instant obliterated by truth, keen, bitter, remorseless, and pinned to its object by wit that was barbed.

Because it does faithfully portray in effective dramatic form and with positive purpose an active phase of social life, the first act of the comedy is entitled to rank as one of the best that Mr. Fitch has ever conceived; but as is always the case with this hard-working young man, all indications of any intention to continue the development of a drama of character fade away by the time the second act is fairly started. As " The Climbers " advanced, Mr. Fitch became concerned merely with the problems of maintaining the action, of developing cunningly a somewhat ordinary and not over and above interesting plot, and of concocting situations with such factors of suspense, appeal, and contrast as should serve to keep the spectators quiet in their seats. In other words, the high-grade comedy, with which he started, began to slide down hill — slowly at first, then faster and faster — into melodrama ; and the end of it all was that most common of all melodramatic episodes, the suicide of the sinning husband, who, after serving the dramatist's purpose as a disturbing element in the story, was shuffled out of the way to make room for the heroine's happiness. Not that these successive downward steps were taken with a rush, — by no means, for had the low level reached toward the end of the play come any sooner than it did, success would never have been secured. One still had the pleasure of recording a second and a third act of much strength and interest, though neither one of them possessed a vestige of the potent drama displayed in the first act. The effectiveness of both was due more to technical skill in developing the situations than to any inherent force in the situations themselves.

The dinner scene, which opened the second act, was a seductive stage picture, and the dark scene which followed, with Sterling's pitiful confession of crime and his frustrated attempt to escape, was daringly original, and, as it happened, really thrilling in its suspense. Strong sentiment, sincerely administered by the players, made the third act go, for no one with a particle of sensibility in his make-up could help sympathising with Warden in his plea in behalf of Mrs. Sterling, whom he had so faithfully and so purely loved. The fact that even the reckless and somewhat soiled Miss Godesby succumbed to it gave the final touch to the sentimental appeal of the episode. Of course it was buncombe, though rather pleasant sort of buncombe, it must be confessed.

With the entrance of the wild-eyed Sterling and his revolver, however, the house of cards began to totter; and while there were moments in the third act when the aunt's pleading and the quiet, stricken wife's praying brought momentary sympathy, — when the pathos was really felt, — in the main, one only waited for the foregone, inevitable conclusion. One knew that Mr. Fitch had written himself into a hole, and there was little more than mild curiosity in watching him somewhat ignominiously crawl out.

Altogether different from "The Climbers" in kind was "Lovers' Lane," a rural drama of pleasing quality, in its lighter moments, — with its serious, though youthful, minister and its nice girl in love with him, its school-children, its mischief-making gossips, and its deacon, — reminding one strongly of Charles

H. Hoyt's " A Midnight Bell." Hoyt's play, however, went more to extremes than did "Lovers' Lane." It was more farcical and more melodramatic. It had a rousing villain, while " Lovers' Lane " had none to speak of. Nor did " A Midnight Bell " touch on sentiment and betrothals except by implication, while " Lovers' Lane " was constantly in the mazes of match-making. Although the plot of Mr. Fitch's play centred continuously around the minister, a very modern type of clergyman, who put a billiard-table in the Boys' Club and favoured card-playing, — although the story of the play was about his courtship of Mary Larkin, his defiance of the prejudices of the townspeople, his loss and his triumphant recovery of his church, — the chief interest in the drama was firmly fixed on one Simplicity Johnson, a most original character study.

Portrayals of children in rural drama are common enough, but most of them are purely farcical conceptions, which cannot be put down as dealing with humanity except in the broadest way. They are crude types, which serve their whole purpose when they arouse hilarious laughter. Simplicity Johnson was

MILLIE JAMES

As Simplicity Johnson in " Lovers' Lane "

not that sort. The character was straight comedy, legitimate comedy as it is termed; it was the representation of a very real and thoroughly understandable little girl. It was extremely keen in its analytical qualities, thoroughly true and sincere both as a conception and as an impersonation, and wonderfully sympathetic in its appeal. I question if Mr. Fitch ever imagined a finer moment or ever struck a truer note than he did in the little scene showing Simplicity's repentance for all the trouble that she had caused her benefactor, the minister. Intensely true was the instinct that made Simplicity yield, not to persuasion or to threats, but in response to the minister's compassionate and sincere love.

Simplicity Johnson was the leading factor in giving "Lovers' Lane" positive character. Without Simplicity the play would have been mildly entertaining, possibly, but on the whole, I am afraid, rather flavourless. Certainly there would have been nothing about it to remember. With Simplicity, however, it was both a unique and an agreeable addition to the list of Fitch dramas.

One of the unpleasant impressions that I

receive from Mr. Fitch's plays is that of exasperation with the dramatist because he does not do better work. I always have the feeling that if only he would take more time, the results achieved would be eminently more worthy. This may be merely a notion of mine. Perhaps he is writing as well as he can. It may be that, knowing how rapidly he works, I assume that his faults are due to careless labour, when as a fact they are temperamental. However that may be, it is true that Mr. Fitch's plays too often lack the finish that leaves one satisfied with the workmanship no matter how little he cares for the product of this workmanship. Now, in " The Way of the World " and " The Girl and the Judge," two plays that seemed to me to fail artistically because they had not been much more than half written, I did like the subject-matter, but I found the plays themselves wearisome and disappointing because chaotically constructed.

" The Way of the World " might be succinctly described as the dramatisation in five acts of an automobile, a scandal, a musicale, a christening, and an election. Some bright individual has called attention to Mr. Fitch's persistency in staging all the social functions — in "The Moth and the Flame" a wedding, in "The Climbers" a funeral, and in "The Way of the World" a christening. The play dealt, primarily, with the fortunes of Mr. and Mrs. Croyden, a loving couple, but childless. Croyden is mixed up in politics. His wife is similarly concerned in society, part of which comprises a rascal named Nevill, for whom she cherishes more than is wise of that dangerous article called sympathy. Between the first and second acts of the play a son and heir is born to the Croydens, also Croyden gets the nomination for governor of the State. Then an ugly scandal pops into the foreground, and Croyden is led to believe that the advent of the child has some connection with his wife's friendship with Nevill. Faced with the scandal, the wife acts foolishly, Nevill lies deliberately in the hope that the dirty rumour will grow big enough to lose Croyden the election, and altogether there is every indication of a dawning divorce suit. But Mrs. Croyden, thoroughly punished for her foolish behaviour, finally has a change of luck. She reunites the divorced Mr. and Mrs. Lake, thereby making them her friends for life. When Croyden interrupts the christening ceremony, refusing to have the child named after him, they fly to her side. Lake takes Croyden away and talks him into a more reasonable mental condition, and Mrs. Lake protects the distracted Mrs. Croyden from gossiping friends, who are intent on still more mischief. By these good offices harmony is restored to the household, and the curtain falls on reconciliation and election, red fire and sky-rockets forming the background for domestic unity and peace.

There were telling bits in the play, one of the best the meeting and reconciliation of the Lakes. The dialogue throughout had considerable smartness, with occasional flashes of wit that brought spontaneous laughter. However, the action of the play as a whole was not perfectly focussed. The drama was entertaining in its episodes, but it lacked oneness and climactic force. The motive for Mrs. Croyden's peculiar attitude toward Nevill was very blind, for her extraordinary childlike innocence regarding men and things was not perceived until she herself declared it when Nevill tried in the last act to get her to elope with him. The noisy climax of the last act — the celebration of the election victory — fell short of effectiveness. It was crowded in so quickly after the meeting between husband and wife that the audience was shocked by the transition from pathos to brass bands.

In "The Girl and the Judge" Mr. Fitch outlined a thoroughly dramatic theme, though he was in too much of a hurry to end his play really to complete it. On one side of the plot is a family of three, — father, mother, and daughter, — and on the other is a youthful judge and his mother. The life of the family of three has been shadowed by the fact that the mother is a kleptomaniac. To save her, the three have been obliged to flee from New York. They have wandered to the Western town where the judge administers justice. It will be understood, of course, that the judge falls in love with the daughter and that their happiness is nearly wrecked by the thieving propensities of the mother. It may be added, too, that a number of interesting, even unusual, characters have been introduced, which liven things up wonderfully. Having said that much, however, there is an end to praise. The play, strong theme and interesting characters notwithstanding, is wholly pointless and tiresome, meandering amid the sweetly sentimental and the slightly effeminate.

An excellent example of the drama's constantly recurring weakness is afforded in the working out of the third act, in which comes the novel situation of the play. The curtain is raised on a bedroom scene. The daughter is heard sobbing in a bed on one side of the stage. The mother, who is in another bed, has stolen a jewel belonging to the judge's mother, and, inasmuch as the judge and the daughter have just become betrothed, the situation is an unpleasant one for the young woman. The act, be it said, is a strong one, with a climax that thrills until it is marred by the unfortunate speech that brings down the curtain. The mother, after making her miserable confession of the theft of the jewel, pleads with the girl not to tell the judge and so ruin her happiness.

"Why must you tell him?" cries the mother.

"Because I love him," pathetically answers the girl, and the curtain falls.

Now that last speech means nothing at all. It is entirely without dramatic power, a sop to sentiment in a situation that demands moral strength and courage. If the girl had made some positive answer such as " Because it is right," how much stronger, how much more inspiring and convincing the effect would have been !

AUGUSTUS THOMAS

Augustus Thomas has been called the dramatist of the States, and it is a fact that, of the four plays which he has written and named after different States, all except one have displayed his best work. Mr. Thomas was born in St. Louis, on January 8, 1859, and after spending six years in the railroad business, he became a special writer and illustrator for St. Louis, Kansas City, and New York newspapers, and finally editor and proprietor of the *Kansas City Mirror*. Then Mr. Thomas turned to the theatre and wrote his first play, a one-act sketch founded on Mrs. Frances Hodgson Burnett's story, " Editha's Burglar," and it was produced with Della Fox as Editha, Mr. Thomas himself as Bill Lewis, the burglar, and W. G. Smythe as Paul Benton. Later the sketch was done in New York with William Gillette as the burglar, and its success there encouraged Mr. Thomas to expand it into three acts. In that form it became one of the first plays in which Edward H. Sothern starred, he playing the burglar, and Elsie Leslie, Editha.

Mr. Thomas's advance to a position in the van of American dramatists dates, however, from the production of his " Alabama," at Palmer's Theatre, New York, on November 2, 1891. It was the first American play that A. M. Palmer had given for a long time, for, like Augustin Daly and Lester Wallack, he had no faith in the native drama. " Alabama " had been in Mr. Palmer's possession for some time. The manager had no especial opinion regarding it, and would never have given it a production had " The Merchant," the play with which he expected to open his season, been ready. To Mr. Palmer's great surprise, " Alabama " gained immediate favour and ran until the next spring. Its quiet sentiment, its delicacy and charm almost poetic, and especially its sweet atmosphere redolent with the fragrance of the magnolia and expressing so sympathetically Southern warmth, chivalry, and humour, were greatly admired. Mr. Thomas has since then written stronger plays than " Alabama," but not one more distinctly beautiful.

Mr. Thomas's other State plays have been " In Mizzoura," " Arizona," and " Colorado," the last the only one in the number written to order and the only one to fail. His other best known works have been, " Man of the World," " Afterthoughts," " The Meddler," " The Man Up-stairs," " Oliver Goldsmith," " On the Quiet," " A Proper Impropriety," " That Overcoat," " The Capitol," and " The Hoosier Doctor."

" Arizona " will serve as an example of the best that Mr. Thomas has offered to the theatre.   Unlike so many American plays, this one is a fine specimen of dramatic construction.   While providing excellently for the eye, it takes full account of dramatic interest and constant and logical development of plot, as well as of vividness and directness of character exposition.   It never stops the action for the sake of a side episode, however dramatic,

or for a trifle of pageantry, however picturesque. "Arizona," it is true, is a melodrama,
but the classification is borne without re-
proach. The play was written for just what
it is and nothing more. There is neither pose
nor insincerity about it. It is a frankly
mechanical work, whose machinery, however,
is artfully concealed by ingenious stagecraft,
whose atmosphere is a faithful reproduction of
Western alkali, breadth, breeziness, and whole-
souled heartiness, and whose characters touch
at every point the realities of human existence.
Without proclaiming any particularly lofty aim,
Mr. Thomas was honest in his work, and gave
forth a play with vitality and force.

Of course, "Arizona" is not the absolute
ideal in dramatic art, — no play that depends
so much on the artifices of the stage can be
termed positively great, — but in its own field
it is an eminently worthy effort. The plot
may be conventional, but even to that a semblance of novelty is given by the very successful transferral to the stage of the locality in
which the action is supposed to pass. The
coherency of the plot is admirable, and its
unfolding intensely dramatic and emotionally

THEODORE ROBERTS
As Canby in "Arizona"

responsive. Mr. Thomas also makes a strong point of his character drawing. His personages are not types. They are individuals carefully defined — Colonel Bonham, stern, self-possessed, but sympathetic, the ideal commanding officer; the fussy Mrs. Canby, narrow, obstinate, and unreasonable to a ridiculous extent, but kind-hearted, just the same, and honest as the day is long; the Mexican vaquero Tony, passionate and sentimental, speaking a dialect of picturesque profanity, of the meaning of which he is innocently unaware; Captain Hodgman, a melodramatic villain undoubtedly, but not so very impossible; Lieutenant Denton, almost too patient and long-suffering for real life, but an attractive youngster notwithstanding; best of all, Canby, the ranchman and stalwart Arizona pioneer, a splendid conception, original and reliant, a portrait abounding in telling contrasts, a man cloaking behind a rough, unpolished exterior, manly chivalry and vigorous sentiment.

The temptation to contrast Clyde Fitch and Augustus Thomas is not to be resisted. They are both young men still, and both are in the front rank of the growing number of American dramatic writers. Temperamentally, however, they are very different, and their work shows this difference in many and varied aspects. Mr. Fitch has the fatal gift of facility. He could dramatise the career of a New Jersey mosquito with fair success, and do it to order at that. Mr. Thomas, on the other hand, is unable apparently to write a really good play by contract and for certain players. He has to develop his dramas with thought independent and free. Mr. Fitch possesses fine skill in placing on the stage the trifles of social life in such lights that they appear important and dramatic. Mr. Thomas does better work in conveying into the theatre a perfect impression of locality. He catches the essential ,peculiarities of sections. As a writer of dialogue Mr. Fitch inclines toward the epigram and intellectual smartness. Mr. Thomas provides only enough talk barely to carry his action. He cuts his sentences down to words, and his words down to single syllables. Finally, Mr. Fitch is not naturally sincere. He is never divorced from a sense of the theatre; his audience is ever in his mind, and he weighs his matter, not in the scales of truth, but in the scales of

theatrical effect. Mr. Thomas is honest,—
except when he tries to write to order. Then
he is more hypocritical and false than Mr.
Fitch ever dreamed were possible.

CHAPTER VII.

CAUSES IN THE AMERICAN THEATRE

HEN Edwin Forrest began his self-imposed task, the object of which was the creating of an enduring American drama, English plays had been presented in this country for over seventy-five years. Not far from 1750 actors from the London theatres first visited the colonies in America, bringing with them complete repertories of the English classics, and, in addition, the latest London successes. The English classics belonged, of course, as much to the English-speaking people in this country as they did to the Englishman who had never left his native land; but the importation of the new plays of the London theatres, welcomed then as they have been welcomed ever since, — for from London have come nearly all of the really satisfactory plays in English, — established a precedent and formed a prejudice that has persisted to this day. The precedent was this: that a play which had made a London success was a play that must of necessity be admirable, and that not to admire it was immediately to write one's self down an ignorant ass. The prejudice was this: that no good thing of a dramatic nature could come from this side of the Atlantic. Thus in the very beginning the American theatre became an echo of the London theatre, and it has remained an echo for a century and a half.

So deep-rooted is the opinion that the citizens of the United States are by the very fact of their citizenship eternally debarred from writing successful plays, that long-winded arguments are propounded every now and then for the single purpose of proving that there is truth concealed somewhere about this false estimate of American literary and dramatic capacity. The claim is made — and not without a show of reason, it must be acknowledged — that environment and education, bustling existence and business engrossment, the hurry and the flurry of deadly competition for material things, have entirely unfitted the American for art production. Given a second thought, however, these conditions will be recognised as purely superficial; and then all derogatory chatter, which would tend to force the conclusion that a people which has produced an Edgar Allan Poe, a Hawthorne, a Washington Irving, and an Emerson, to say nothing of innumerable lesser lights that have worked and are working in the service of letters, is not able to bring forth at least one worthy dramatist, will be rightly classed as nonsense. Still, let the natural capacity be ever so great, it will not come to its richest fruition — unless, indeed, it is brought to perfection by the presence in unlimited power of supreme genius — except it be given encouragement and sympathetic attention; and the contention that conditions in the United States are not now, — in fact, never have been, — favourable to the quick growth of a native drama is true. It would have been bad enough if the American drama had been obliged to struggle against indifference alone; but, as a matter of fact, to attain the little recognition that it has received, it has had to fight active and almost malicious aversion, manifested in the greatest measure by the more refined and intellectual classes of the community, by persons who have flattered their vanity with the Pharisaical pose, "I am better than thou." By such, the American drama has been literally kicked out of the back door; but, fortunately, they cannot prevent it from reëntering by the front windows the instant that a beckoning finger declares that the time for reëntering has come.

When one is tempted to fret over the slow growth of the native drama, it may ease anxious thought to remember that the theatre did not become prominent in the United States till about the time that the effects of the French Renaissance were being felt in the English theatre. Not only did the growing American theatre quickly absorb the meagre supply of English drama sent to it from London, but at the same time it assiduously secured for its delectation everything that prolific France had to offer. Small wonder that, in the face of all this competition, the American dramatic weakling did not thrive and become vigorous. Spasmodic attempts to "do something" for the American drama there occasionally were, notably by Forrest and Lawrence Barrett; but the time was not ripe in their day for their work to receive either the appreciation or the support that it fairly earned. They were handicapped by having to depend for patronage on a public which cared nothing for the ideals that Forrest and Barrett represented, and they were sneered at by managers, who systematically discouraged their worthier ambitions.

Theatrical conditions in the United States are peculiar, and by their peculiarity they give the manager so much authority that his sneer becomes a matter of decided importance. On it, in fact, hangs the fate of the American drama, and because of it the American drama is lagging behind the world. The United States has no natural artistic centre, where there is to be found a concentrated and a consistent public taste, refined and cultivated, catholic but discriminating, which must be acknowledged and satisfied. We have no Paris, no Berlin, no London. The business centre of our theatre is New York, and the attempt is generally made to establish New York as the artistic centre of the drama as well. But an artistic centre is not made by spending money in advertising and shouting, " Here shall it be." An artistic centre is the result of natural selection. New York is the largest city in the United States, but it is no more the representative city than is Chicago or Philadelphia or Boston. In fact, as regards the specific art division of the drama, New York is of all places the one least likely to judge fairly, for the reason that its vast numbers of theatregoers belong to a considerable extent to a great floating population. This theatrical public is made up of men and women who are temporarily in New York for the express purpose of having a good time; and with them, to have a good time in New York means to patronise a Weber and Fields show, or some even more nonsensical musical burletta, which is uncompromisingly strong in the number of its attractive young women and unblushingly weak in everything else.

The United States is the land of the theatrical circuit, and that fact gives the manager here control of a definite sphere. The business of the theatrical company is complicated by the continual shifting from place to place, by the exigencies of travel, by the necessity of jumping from one theatre to another and of appearing before differing publics, by the

countless number of details that hinge on
these vacillating conditions. Comparatively
speaking, it is not such a difficult task to
supervise the workings of a permanent theatre
in London, where patronage, more or less
steady and determined, can be counted upon;
but the management of a theatrical company
in the United States, where nothing is certain
or calculable, is intricate work. In London
the manager is safe in turning over the details
of his business to a subordinate. He is then
left free to devote some thought to what
goes on his stage. Because this is possible,
the English actor has been able to carry the
responsibility of both managing and acting
without undue strain. In this country, however, the manager, instead of thinking about
art, must puzzle out the mysteries of time-
tables. He must be an expert on railroad
rates and routes, on hotels, and on theatres.
With all this wearying detail of so much importance, and bearing so directly on the success
of the enterprise, few actors care to try both
acting and managing; and few managers have
the time, even if they have the inclination, to
bother much about the quality of their produc-

tions. The balance sheet at the close of each performance is their only critical standard as well as the only critical opinion in which they are the least interested; for the American manager is primarily a man of business, with his thought firmly fixed on the dollars. The mercenary thought and the art ideal are like oil and water — they do not mix.

However, one must not make the mistake of holding each and every theatre manager personally responsible for the odd state of mind that makes him invariably slight the highest welfare of the stage whenever the question of additional bit of coin in the box-office is concerned. The theatre manager, in company with men and women of all walks of life, is the bewildered and ignorant victim of the uncompromising battle between materialism and idealism, a battle that will last as long as any taint of materialism remains undestroyed. " The love of money," say the Scriptures, " is the root of all evil;" and it is the love of money that is raising the mischief, not only in the American theatre, but also in every line of American activity. It is the domination of the commercial manager and the commercial

spirit in the American theatre that is responsible for the dearth of American drama, and
for every other shortcoming that is attached
to the American stage.

Progress is the sure result of inspired and
original thought. Progress implies sacrifice
of the present for the promised reward of the
future. There is no real progress possible for
selfish commercialism. The man who is working only for money is hidebound by prejudice
and superstition. He is a timid traveller of
unexplored regions, fearful of the future, and
easily frightened by shadows, which more often
than not are the creatures of his fears. He
is by instinct a follower, and not a leader.
The money-maker is the slave of habit; his
ideas range only in narrow and familiar
channels. When the money-maker happens
to be managing a theatre, he likes to believe
that he is holding his fingers on the pulse of
the public, ready to catch the faintest flicker-
ing throb; but in this he is entirely mistaken.
The commercial manager would fain believe
that, if he is not forming public taste, he is at
least marching abreast of it in a painstaking
endeavour to live up to his lofty ideal of

"giving the public what it wants." The commercial manager deceives himself with sophistries and platitudes. He does not gauge public opinion, but he follows tradition. Now tradition is being constantly outgrown, and this essential mark of a progressive people causes the commercial manager great worriment. He is continually finding himself behind the times. Driven desperate by the repeated warnings of disconcerting failures, he at length tremblingly pursues some struggling and adventurous originator into the frightful mazes of the unknown. Finding there a popular success, the commercial manager is nonplussed and astounded that the public, to which he had been catering so devotedly in the old way, should devour with avidity his strange dish. Perplexed beyond reasoning, he forthwith declares the theatrical business a lottery. The commercial manager has strongly developed a faculty for falling into the fallacy of the universal, and there he flounders in a pitifully helpless fashion. Because a certain brand of theatrical entertainment proves to be acceptable in one instance, he eagerly embraces the conclusion that a like brand of entertainment will be acceptable on all occasions. He works that brand until it nauseates the public. Patronage at last ceases, and again the commercial manager is left in vague and startled wonderment at the fickleness of the public.

Let me re-state succinctly these important facts regarding the American theatre. The drama came to the United States from England, and English influence has always been paramount in the development of the American theatre. No sooner, however, did the theatre become firmly established in this country, and the time arrive when the American play in the ordinary course of things was due, than the Frenchmen of the Renaissance began to supply the world, including the English theatre, with plays. From England first, and then from France direct, these plays were brought to America, and so much did they excel the first feeble attempts at dramatic writing in this country that the inevitable prejudice against the new, which was inspired by the American play, was forthwith expanded into violent antipathy against the American play in all shapes, forms, and places. The fact that the drama in America has no home, and that all theatrical companies here must travel, has made the theatrical manager a peculiar necessity — so much of a necessity that it is the manager with his strong commercialism, and not the actor, who alone is dependent upon the art of the theatre for thorough satisfaction in his work, that has been for years the ruling factor in the American playhouse. Because the manager is commercial, and therefore unprogressive, he has retained predominant in his consciousness the many-years-old prejudice against the American play; and because he is without imagination or intuition, robbed of both by his beloved materialism, and, thus bereft, is unable to judge the trend of public opinion and to meet it and guide it before it has had time fully to express itself, the commercial manager has failed, even at this late day, to realise that there is in reality no prejudice against the American play; that, on the contrary, what the public, ignorant itself of its own desires, actually does want is thoroughly American drama, picturing familiar conditions and characters, and deducing from these inspiring lessons of truth.

Only a perfunctory reference to historical

fact is required to prove the assertion that the slow development of the American drama has been due to the fact that the American theatre has always been used primarily to secure a money profit for the American manager. Apply the following testimony by Dion Boucicault regarding the English theatre of half a century ago to the American theatre of to-day, and the condition of affairs in the American theatre will be exactly approximated.

" For example," wrote Mr. Boucicault, " the usual price received by Sheridan Knowles, Bulwer, and Talfourd for their plays was £500. I was a beginner in 1841, and received for my comedy, ' London Assurance,' £300. For that amount the manager bought the privilege of playing the work for his season. Three years later I offered a new play to a principal London theatre. The manager offered me £100 for it. In reply to my objection to the smallness of the sum he remarked, ' I can go to Paris and select a first-class comedy; having seen it performed, I feel certain of its effect. To get this comedy translated will cost me £25. Why should I give you £300 or £400 for your comedy, of the success of which I cannot feel

so assured ? ' The argument was unanswerable
and the result inevitable. I sold a work for
£100 that took me six months' hard work to
compose, and accepted a commission to translate three French plays at £50 apiece. This
work afforded me child's play for a fortnight.
Thus the English dramatist was obliged either
to relinquish the stage altogether or to become
a French copyist."

Substitute for the manager's statement, " I
can go to Paris," the declaration, " I can go to
London," and the argument of the American
manager is exactly stated. As Dion Boucicault said, it is unanswerable, for no man would
offer such an argument, unless he were working strictly on a money basis, with no regard
either for art or for ethics.

As has been noted in a previous chapter,
the ruling influence in the America theatre
for many years was Wallack, father and son.
The elder Wallack was an English actor and
naturally disposed to favour English dramatic
products, and Lester Wallack followed unfal-
teringly his father's footsteps. It is reported
by many that it was almost an impossibility to
get Lester Wallack to read, much less to pro-

duce, an American play. Occasionally, when the pressure became too strong for him decently to resist, Wallack would bring out an American play, thereby proving, to his own satisfaction at least, the reasonableness of his contention that American plays were worthless; for when he did produce an American play, Wallack had a faculty of making it the worst American play that his collection contained. Naturally it failed. Wallack knew that it would fail before he put it in rehearsal, and the failure gave him still another argument against bothering with the American drama.

Augustin Daly was only a trifle better than Wallack, notwithstanding the fact that one of his first and biggest successes was Bronson Howard's " Saratoga." Daly opened his first Fifth Avenue Theatre on August 16, 1869, with Tom Robertson's " Play," following it six weeks later with Boucicault's " London Assurance." The American premier of Sardou's " Frou-Frou " occurred at this theatre on January 15, 1870. The opening attraction of the season of 1870–71 was " Man and Wife," dramatised from a Wilkie Collins novel; and " Saratoga," Daly's first American play, was given on

December 21. The next two leading Daly productions were " Divorce "(1871) and " L'Article 47 " (1872), both from the French. This theatre was burned on January 1, 1873, and Daly opened the Worrell Sisters' Theatre three weeks later as Daly's New Fifth Avenue. The attraction was " Alixe," from the French. The following December Daly abandoned this house and leased what had been the St. James Theatre, naming that the Fifth Avenue. The first play was James Albery's " Fortune," which failed, and the old comedies were revived until " Parricide " gave Ada Dyas, on December 17, a chance to make her American début.

Daly productions of new plays for about twenty-five years were as follows, all from foreign sources except the three or four that are noted as American: " Folline," " Charity," " Moorcroft," by Bronson Howard (American), " Women of the Day," " The Big Bonanza," " Our Boys," " New Leah," " Pique," " Life," " The American " (Daly adaptation of " L'Estrangère "), Bronson Howard's " Wives " (American), " The Way We Live," " Our First Families," by Edgar Fawcett (American),

" Needles and Pins," " Cinderella at School," " American Abroad," by Edgar Fawcett (American), " The Passing Regiment," " Odette," " Mankind," " The Squire," " Our English Friend," " Serge Panine," " 7–20–8," " Dollars and Sense," " Boys and Girls," " Lords and Commons," " Love on Crutches," " A Night Off," " Denise," " The Magistrate," " Nancy & Co.," " Dandy Dick," " Railroad of Love," " Lottery of Love," " An International Match," " Samson and Delilah," " Golden Widow," " The Great Unknown," " A Priceless Paragon," " The Wooden Spoon," " The Prayer," " New Lamps for Old," " The Prodigal Son," " The Cabinet Minister," " Love in Tandem," and during the last Daly seasons, " Cyrano de Bergerac " and " The Great Ruby."

This list by no means includes all of the Daly productions, but it does contain practically all of the really important new plays. The list is certainly sufficiently complete to make it plain that Mr. Daly did not plunge very heavily on the American drama.

The next of the great producing managers in this country was A. M. Palmer. He was more fortunate in his ventures with the American drama than was Mr. Daly, yet Mr. Palmer came to regard American plays with almost as much indifference as did Lester Wallack. The success of " Alabama " was the greatest surprise Mr. Palmer ever had. For week in and week out he had been producing English plays, and they had failed one after another until the manager was forced into giving Mr. Thomas's despised work a chance. It proved both a financial and an artistic triumph. Mr. Palmer became manager of the Union Square Theatre, New York, in the fall of 1872. " Agnes," a comedy by Sardou, was his first venture, and it proved an immediate success, running one hundred nights. For the next season Mr. Palmer formed a stock company. It was a bold stroke, for three stock companies already existed in New York — Wallack's in high comedy, Booth's in tragedy, and Daly's in lighter comedy and farce of French and German adaptation.

Mr. Palmer gathered together a company capable of idealising the romantic school of the drama, and made his first sensational success with Hart Jackson's adaptation of D'Ennery's and Carmon's " The Two Orphans," produced on December 21, 1874. In the stock company at that time were Kate Claxton, Clara Morris, Maude Granger, Rose Eytinge, Meta Bartlett, Kate Holland, Charles R. Thorne, Jr., Stuart Robson, and Mr. and Mrs. McKee Rankin. For ten years Mr. Palmer guided the fortunes of the Union Square, rarely meeting with misadventure, and sticking to the end to foreign plays, notwithstanding the fact that one of his noteworthy successes was Bronson Howard's "The Banker's Daughter." His chief Union Square productions were "The Geneva Cross," "Rose Michel," "A Celebrated Case," "Ferrial," "Miss Multon," "The Danicheffs," "Smike," "Pink Dominoes," "Olivia," "Mother and Son," "My Partner" (American), "French Flats," and "Lights o' London."

In September, 1884, Mr. Palmer joined with the Mallory brothers in the management of the Madison Square Theatre, and there he recorded half a dozen years of brilliant achievement. It was, however, the remarkable Madison Square Theatre company, rather than the plays that were given, which brought such reputation to the house; and in this company were such splendid players as Agnes Booth, W. J. LeMoyne, Fred Robinson, Herbert Kelcey, Harry M. Pitt, Jessie Millward, Annie Russell, Maud Harrison, J. H. Stoddart, E. M. Holland, Marie Burroughs, C. P. Flockton, and Louis Massen. The first Madison Square production, with which Mr. Palmer was connected, was "The Private Secretary." In March, 1885, Mr. Palmer took complete control of the theatre, bringing out on April 13 following, "Sealed Instructions," by Mrs. Julia Campbell Ver Planck. There came, during successive seasons, "Saints and Sinners," "Engaged," "Old Love Letters," by Bronson Howard, "Marjory's Lovers," by Brander Matthews, "Elaine," from Tennyson, by George Parsons Lathrop and Harry Edwards, "Jim the Penman," "A Parisian Romance," "Heart of Hearts," "Partners," "Captain Swift," with Augustus Thomas's "The Man of the World" as a curtain raiser, "The Burglar," by Thomas, "Sunlight and Shadow," "Aftermath," and Thomas's "Alabama."

In 1890 Mr. Palmer removed his company to Wallack's Theatre, which he renamed Palmer's Theatre, opening the house with

" Alabama," and later installing there Edward S. Willard, who, on his first visit to this country, was remarkably successful with " The Middleman " and " Judah." Mr. Palmer's leading productions at this theatre were " The Broken Seal," by Sidney Grundy, " Colonel Carter of Cartersville," " Aristocracy," by Bronson Howard, " Mercedes," by Thomas Bailey Aldrich, and " Lady Windemere's Fan," by Oscar Wilde. During these last years, Mr. Palmer did not find his theatrical ventures profitable, and he gradually became so involved financially that not even the Paul Potter dramatisation of DuMaurier's " Trilby," which ran for nearly two years in New York, could save him. Of recent years he has been quite content to pass a quiet existence as Richard Mansfield's manager. Unquestionably Mr. Palmer was more receptive to the American drama than either Lester Wallack or Mr. Daly. Mr. Palmer's final failure was the result of too strong competition in the theatrical business. He could not get plays abroad, and he could not get them at home. Mr. Palmer was an eminently intelligent manager, but he was conservative. The plunger had entered the theat-

rical field, and it was his policy quickly to grab everything in sight. The just-a-trifle-slow and just-a-trifle-old-fashioned manager like Mr. Palmer had to go to the wall.

Mr. Palmer's place with Mr. Daly at the head of the New York theatre was taken by Daniel Frohman, who had climbed into prominence on the back of the American play. He was first heard of at the Madison Square Theatre, where he helped to make " Hazel Kirke " a valuable property, and to place " Young Mrs. Winthrop," " Esmeralda," " The Rajah," and " May Blossom " before the public. All these were American plays. In 1886 Daniel Frohman took the Lyceum Theatre off Steele Mackaye's hands, organising the Lyceum Theatre company, which in due season became an important and worthy New York institution. It was headed by Herbert Kelcey and Georgia Cayvan, and included at first Henry Miller, Nelson Wheatcroft, Mr. and Mrs. Charles Walcot, W. J. LeMoyne, Charles Dickson, Grace Henderson, and Mrs. Thomas Whiffen. Later William Faversham succeeded Mr. Miller, and still later Fritz Williams, Katherine Florence, and Elizabeth

Tyree became important members. One of Mr. Frohman's early ventures was the starring of E. H. Sothern in " The Highest Bidder," rewritten from a comedy by Madison Morton called " Trade." The first successes of the Lyceum Theatre company were the two American plays, " The Wife " and " The Charity Ball," both by Henry C. DeMille and David Belasco. Therewith, however, practically ended Mr. Frohman's American productions, though the circumstance that he substituted for them the plays of Arthur Wing Pinero and Henry Arthur Jones, and saw to it that they were acted in this country fully as well and sometimes a little better than they were in London, earned for Mr. Frohman sincere gratitude, and kept him at the head of American producers of first-class modern drama.

Reference to Daniel Frohman naturally brings to mind that exceedingly energetic member of the same family, Charles Frohman, who by ceaseless endeavour has pushed himself into a leading place among American theatre managers. It was an American play also that gave Charles Frohman a chance to blossom into a magnate of far-reaching influence.   When Bronson Howard's "Shenandoah" was produced at the Boston Museum, on November 18, 1888, it was seen by Mr. Frohman, who was stranded in Boston, financially cleaned out and without an idea of what the future had in store for him.   The play was not at first a great success, but Mr. Frohman thought that it had possibilities, and the correctness of that judgment was the making of the manager.   He secured the rights to present the play outside of Boston, and not having any money, he took as partners Al Hayman, who then controlled the great western circuits, and R. W. Hooley. Frohman put on the play in spectacular fashion at the Star Theatre, New York, two of the partners advancing $1,500 apiece, and Frohman giving his time and labour.   Three years later the three had divided $140,000 in profits, and Bronson Howard had received $100,000 in royalties.   That combination in 1889 of Charles Frohman with Al Hayman was the infant grasp of the so-called Theatrical Syndicate, to-day the leading factor in the American theatre.

The Theatrical Syndicate is a frankly commercial enterprise, making no pretences of devotion to art except in so far as art brings a sure profit. The Syndicate is chiefly embarrassed by the scarcity of original plays, to cover which it has resorted to the dramatisation of novels and the making of stars of players hardly worthy of the honour. One prominent reason for the scarcity of plays arises from the circumstance that the Syndicate will not experiment with dramas that do not promise a certain success. Aside from the myriad offerings of Clyde Fitch, and of plays written on contract by a few others, the work of the American dramatist is not considered. English and French dramas that have succeeded abroad are given the preference on the ground that they are safer investments, and that in producing them there is avoided the responsibility of backing one's own art judgment. Nor are any foreign plays tried, unless their money value is evident and determined. Thus it has happened that, although the poetical dramas of Stephen Phillips have been attracting more attention in London during the last few seasons than the works of any other English dramatist, not one of these

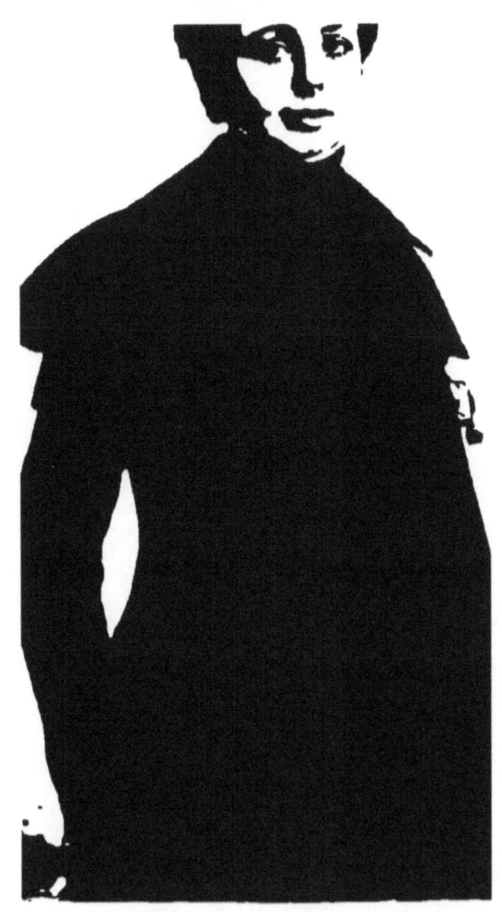

MAUDE ADAMS

As the Duke of Reichstadt in " L'Aiglon."

plays has been given an American production. Their financial success in this country is regarded as doubtful. The same thing is true as regards the serious plays of the Continental dramatists, only four of which have received regular productions in recent seasons, — Henri Lavedan's " Catherine," produced by Charles Frohman for Annie Russell; Gerhart Hauptmann's " Die Versunkene Glocke," into the production of which E. H. Sothern put his own money; Edmond Rostand's " Cyrano de Bergerac," brought out by Richard Mansfield on his own responsibility; and Rostand's " L'Aiglon," acted by Maude Adams under the auspices of Charles Frohman, after Sarah Bernhardt had made her impersonation of the Eaglet a Parisian sensation. Looking upon the theatre as strictly a business enterprise, the last thing thought of by the commercial manager, when the matter of producing a new play is being discussed, is the question of art. Dramatic values are determined entirely on a cash basis. It does not, therefore, require either argument or figures to make it plain that so thoroughly materialistic a method cannot fail in the long run to lower definitely that artistic endeavour to which it is applied.

The combination, consisting of Nixon and Zimmermann of Philadelphia, Klaw and Erlanger, Hayman and Charles Frohman, all of New York, was first heard of during the season of 1895–96. Under its control at that time had come about forty theatres, which the Syndicate had agreed to provide with attractions, guaranteeing each a succession of first-class companies, and taking in return a percentage for the booking as well as the usual percentage for the company itself. The strength of the Syndicate lay, not in the fact that it controlled all the theatres of the country, — that would have made it altogether too cumbersome, — but in the fact that it controlled sections, so that companies travelling from one point to another were forced into Syndicate houses in order to escape long and expensive jumps that would quickly have depleted profits. Thus New Orleans was cut off from the North, not because the Syndicate had all the New Orleans theatres, but because it controlled theatres in which companies on the way to and from New Orleans were obliged to play. The same conditions existed as regards other cities South and West.

Even as commercialism brought the Syndicate into existence, so commercialism kept it alive and finally handed over to it almost unlimited power. At first the opposition to the combination was strong, prominent actors being particularly hostile to it. Had this opposition continued steadfast, there is little question that in a comparatively short time it would have broken the trust. The Syndicate, however, did not attack these opponents as a body — that would have had the effect of drawing the antagonistic interests closer together in the face of a common enemy. The Syndicate dealt individually with those who had manifested discontent. It offered such actors as it considered the backbone of the opposition extra inducements in the way of bookings, longer engagements in New York, and other things dear to the player's heart. Although the original agreement to stand fast against the trust had been signed by Francis Wilson, James A. Herne, James O'Neill, Richard Mansfield, and Mrs. Fiske, when the season ended in the spring of 1898, only Mrs. Fiske and Francis Wilson remained outside the Syndicate. In January, 1899, Wilson succumbed. In 1900, Henrietta Crosman joined Mrs. Fiske, and at the end of the season of 1902, James K. Hackett was added to the number, the three forming a new body for the booking of attractions independent of the trust. Of course, there have been from the first prominent managers outside of the Syndicate, such as Liebler and Company, William A. Brady, Kirke LaShelle, and Henry W. Savage; but they have been content to dwell in peace with the powers, placing their attractions with the Syndicate and paying the price, when they had a success, and going it alone as best they could when their offerings were not regarded as worth while by the Syndicate booking office.

The child of dissatisfaction, bred of the American theatre, is rapidly growing into the adult of positive demand. Everywhere, those with ears that hear and intelligence that comprehends, recognise the call for something new. Even the impassive purveyor of theatrical attractions is conscious of it and struggles mightily to understand. But his wits are dulled by the clink of gold, and he cannot fathom the mystery.

What is this strange, new thing? Not the French farce; that is dead and buried. Not the dramatised novel; that is dying, if not already dead. Not fresh importations of London successes, though for them we are grateful, for they are the best of the new that we get. None of these. The demand is for the American play. We are tired of lords and ladies, good, bad, and indifferent; we are tired of rural dramas; we are tired of bombastic romance; we are tired of false sentiment, of false farce with a foreign heritage, of false melodrama with no heritage at all. We want truth; we want honest comedy of American society — I do not mean by society the meagre body dubbed the "four hundred" — and impressive tragedy of American life. We want dramas that declare to us with fidelity and with insight the world we know, as it is and as it should be.

And the truth will come. When the demand for it reaches a full climax of insistence and power, the man to meet the demand will arise, fully equipped for the fray, with sling in hand prepared to slay the Philistine. It has always been so from the beginning, and it is so now. I do not think that this champion is writing plays to-day. He is not Clyde Fitch, unstable and flighty, an untrustworthy faddist racing madly after unknown gods. Nor is he the present Augustus Thomas, worthy, indeed, while the inspiration is on, but ever striving for quantity to the detriment of quality. Neither Fitch nor Thomas have the sound balance, the spiritual force, the mental grasp, and the sturdiness of conviction needed by the pioneer. Their emotion is too conscious of self to be spontaneous, vigorous, and unabashed. Their ideas of life are too conventional to cut to the bone. The man — for it will be a man — to bring to us the American drama, for which we are so impatiently waiting, will have courage, power, simplicity, sincerity, earnestness, and honesty. Verily there is need of such a man. Moreover, when he does come, he will be recognised — no doubt of that.

CHAPTER VIII.

HE especial variety of frayed, feminine emotion, which found its foremost exponent in this country in the Clara Morris of the seventies, was purely French in its derivation, the aftermath of the sentimental triumph of " La Dame aux Camellias," by Alexandre Dumas, *fils*. Notwithstanding that the vogue of " Camille," which amply set forth the peculiar social status of Marguerite Gautier, might make it so appear, Dumas's play was not in any definite way responsible for the English drama of the fallen woman. This drama, which so vigorously declared itself during the last decade of the nineteenth century, — the drama of Oscar Wilde, Sidney Grundy, and Arthur Wing Pinero, — was not French even by descent. It was brought into being as a reflection of definable conditions in English social life, conditions which the stage probably exaggerated, but which, however, it did not absolutely falsify. There is the bitter cynicism of sin against the conscience in this English drama, cynicism such as is never felt in the French drama, of which the social outcast is a leading figure.

Indeed, the difference between the two dramas is the difference between hypocrisy and between matter-of-fact and shameless recognition of a thing that is regarded as a necessity and, therefore, as only conventionally bad. The English drama presents the impure woman as wrapping herself in a cloak of virtuous conduct, not desirous of being good, but mortally afraid lest her wickedness be found out; the French drama presents the woman as frankly a harlot, who has sinned and suffered, but who does not masquerade under false colours. Thus the diverging temperaments of the two nations have clearly affected their respective dramas. No one would deny that the bad Englishman is just as bad as the bad Frenchman; but even a bad Englishman has bred in his bones the Calvinistic conscience, and that cannot be gotten rid of in a single generation. It may not keep the Englishman from misbehaving, but it, at least, makes him self-conscious of his vice and fearful of being found out in his sin. He dreads a scandal. This is, of course, decidedly negative morality, but it assuredly has some very positive results. The Englishman may sin, but he is not able entirely to fool himself into believing that his sins are really virtues. He is not ready publicly to parade evil as something necessary and, therefore, to be in a measure condoned. The Englishman has not yet brought himself to the point of licensing social evil, and thereby legalising it, as the Frenchman has done and as he has praised himself for doing.

The Calvinistic conscience, working on the dramatic theme of the fallen woman, has resulted in a drama, the effect of which — if it really has any decided moral effect one way or the other — must be on the side of virtue. It is, therefore, amusingly paradoxical that against no modern drama has the charge of immorality been so persistently brought as it has against the English drama dealing with the sex problem. It seems to me a self-evident proposition that a play like "Camille," which is specifically the justification of the harlot, is immeasurably more dangerous to the morals of the " young person," than a play like " The Second Mrs. Tanqueray," which preaches un- relentingly the sermon that " the wages of sin is death." Yet " Camille " is passed by as a matter of course, while " The Second Mrs. Tanqueray " causes a shudder every time that it is presented. The nub of the matter lies in the fact that a play like " The Second Mrs. Tanqueray " boldly uncovers evil so that no one can help seeing that it is evil, while a play like " Camille " cunningly conceals evil and even tries to make it seem good. " Camille " is deceptive. It glosses vice with the sugar- coating of sentimentality. It deliberately fo- cuses all the sympathy on Marguerite Gautier. The sin for which she suffers is adroitly hidden from .view, while the suffering itself is dragged into the foreground, a spectacle for the tearful contemplation of the emotionally susceptible. A paradox indeed, when those weep for a Marguerite Gautier in a play, who in life would be too overwhelmed with horror and aversion to extend the helping hand that might save a human Marguerite Gautier actually worth weeping over! Thus "Camille," gently erasing evil with soft insinuation and mild depreciation, makes truth false even to the elect, who declare such a beautiful play harmless, if not positively edifying and ennobling.

But how different the attitude toward a play like "The Second Mrs. Tanqueray," which commits the offence of shocking settled humanity with a plain statement of fact, which dares to strip the mask from the mystery of iniquity and thus rob it of its false attractiveness and claim of allurement and pleasure! The effect of "The Second Mrs. Tanqueray" is indeed that of horror and disgust; but it is a mistaken notion of things that causes the hue and cry of immorality to be raised against a play which shows evil in its true light. At best, the issue with Mr. Pinero for writing such a drama is one of taste, and not of morals. It is not evil that horrifies and disgusts which is really dangerous; but it is evil which presents itself in the disguise of good, as something desirable and fascinating, as a relief from the monotony of righteousness and as a bringer of zest and joy to life and experience.

The ethics of the French social drama, from "Camille" to "Zaza," argue in favour of the following dangerous proposition — that, should the unfortunate and embarrassing condition arise, which places a man in a position where he has to decide between his wife and his mistress, it is his chivalrous duty to choose his mistress. The reason presented is this: that the wife does not need his protection, that she is in the right from the world's view-point and has the law on her side; that the mistress, on the other hand, has sacrificed everything to passion, that she stands legally and morally condemned without either hearing or defence, that the least the man for whom she has risked so much can do, is to stand by her unflinchingly. The error in this plausible proposition is a subtle one, and it has led many into the false position of upholding the man who has thus stood by "the woman he has wronged," and of accepting him as a "thorough gentleman," bravely unconventional and heroically unselfish. Especially high does he mount the pinnacle, if only the wife, whom he has tossed aside, be shown in an unattractive and unlovely light, as cold or unsympathetic or bent on separating two loving hearts that fain would beat as one. It is so easy, when questions of right and wrong are being argued from one point of view only, to be satisfied with superficial considerations instead of digging down deep for. fundamentals and building the structure of agreement or disagreement on a solid basis.

It is scarcely necessary to argue for the purity of the marriage relation. It is self-evident that, without moral regulations, it would be impossible to sustain the complications of social and communal relations; and it is also self-evident that there is no moral regulation more inherently important or more generally effective in its practical workings than the regulation of marriage. Indeed, the French emotional drama does not directly attack marriage as an institution, any further than to declare, what everybody knows, that it is by no means ideally perfect; but the French drama works more subtly by placing the so-called rights of the individual in opposition to the rights of the community as expressed and enforced in the marriage law. This move is both plausible and appealing, for the unhappy and misguided marriage is too common to escape

any one's attention.   Ignoring the direct cause
for all connubial failures, namely, animal passion and personal selfishness, the French drama
proposes to remedy difficulties by bringing
into the case the still further complications
engendered by deceit, disloyalty, and dis-
honour.

It is a fundamental fact that right is right,
that wrong is wrong, and that wrong never
makes right.   Yet the whole argument of the
French " wife-and-mistress " drama rests on the
assertion that, under certain conditions, two
wrongs may make a right.   Naturally, this
argument is not thus bluntly stated — to do
so would be to make it immediately ridiculous;
but, befogged though it be by untoward circumstances, by twists and turns of sympathy
and sentiment, it none the less calls for the
acceptance of the impossible; it advances the
false claim that evil can result in good.

Everybody acknowledges the wickedness and
the misery of the unhappy and the uncongenial
marriage.   Everybody desires a solution of the
problem involved in such a marriage.   But no
one who is sanely minded can regard as an
adequate solution the course of conduct offered

by the French drama, a course the inevitable results of which are further wrong-doing, further misery, and further degrading entanglements. Instead of relieving the irksome bonds of those unfittingly yoked together, the counsel of the French dramatists is to take on other bonds, which are not only equally as irksome, but which carry with them the added burden of shame and dishonesty, bonds which force the breaking of solemn vows, the disregarding of the law of the state and the rights of the individual, which mean the sacrificing of uprightness for the gratification of the desire of the moment. For, reduced to its lowest terms, the motive of all illicit love is either brutalising animalism or none the less brutalising selfishness.

Pictured thus in the bright sunlight of the open, with the issue and conclusion unclouded by the personalities of players or the subtilties of playwrights, the turn in the road, at which the French drama goes astray, seems evident enough ; but in the theatre, — where every sort of combination, complication, and diverting device is used to attract the attention from the ethical axiom, that two wrongs do not make a right, — the keeping of one's judgment free, open, and unbiassed will be found by no means so easy a matter. To perceive how slyly vice is made to bedeck itself in the robes of virtue, let the play " Zaza," the latest of this class of drama, be submitted to the merest modicum of critical analysis. In the first place, it may be noted that, before the curtain goes up, one is soothed by the ingratiating fact that the heroine is played by the star actress. Thus, as an important preliminary, before a word is uttered, or a situation revealed, the fallen woman becomes an object of stimulated interest and even sympathetic attention. The interest thus aroused is further increased by the colourful spectacle of the first act, which also serves to accentuate the coarseness and the salaciousness of the Zaza who is not yet " reformed by love."

It is in the second act that sentimentality begins fairly to work. One is introduced immediately to a billing and cooing breakfast scene, which depicts Zaza and her companion thoroughly under the mesmeric sway of sensual passion. Zaza's great devotion to her man is marked, and with emphasis it is indicated how vastly she has improved under his influence or rather under the influence of her "love" for him. Already she is less coarse and more womanly. She has abandoned all her promiscuous amours. She is good indeed, "reformed by love." Having thus pushed her into vantage-ground from which it is safe to offer her as a martyr to be pitied, harrowing emotionalism is inaugurated. Zaza learns that she has been deceived. Her man has a wife, and, therefore, the next step toward the sanctification of the heroine is to bring Zaza and the wife face to face. This accomplished, one is invited to note the contrast — the wife cool, dispassionate, and colourless; Zaza, "poor Zaza," sobbing, broken-hearted, and totally undone. Finally comes the crowning episode that completes the conquest of the susceptible — Zaza instantly won from her intent of vengeance by the prattle of innocent childhood, and nobly sacrificing her great happiness that a cloud may not mar the serenity of the man she loves. Is it not all irresistibly lovely? Can you wonder that "Zaza" played steadily to crowded houses for two seasons?

The primary purpose of this statement regarding the French emotional drama has not been to reveal the inherent immorality of both its theme and its treatment of that theme. That phase of the matter could have been disposed of in short order, if it had been thought necessary to pay even that much attention to it. What I have purposed showing is the essentially false premise of all plays of the " Camille " and " Zaza " type, and the inherent dishonesty of all dramatists who choose to deal with the theme utilised in such plays; and, having stated this falsehood, I wish to emphasise the positive and convincing conclusion that there can be no real nor genuine art in a class of drama that is essentially false and dishonest. It should be held as an undeviating principle that art, which is the perfect expression of the good, the true, and the beautiful, can neither lie itself nor be utilised to declare a lie; that a play which presents erroneous conclusions deduced from false premises is not art; that anything which, while working for evil and while inharmonious with truth and the highest ideal of good, poses as art, is a usurper and should never be permitted to occupy the position that it arrogantly and impudently claims for itself.

CLARA MORRIS

Born in Canada of Irish parents, reared in poverty, with neither social nor educational advantages, starting in the theatre as a ballet girl when scarcely more than a child, beginning first with the smallest of parts and gradually working upward from low comedy characters and juveniles to the position of leading woman, at length achieving in an instant, and that, too, when barely twenty-one years old, recognition as the foremost emotional actress on the American stage, the career of Clara Morris stands unparalleled for striking dramatic contrast. When, moreover, one adds to the sensation of her achievements the acknowledged fact that the temperamental force of her acting and the magnetic appeal of her personality were sufficient, when exercised upon the most cultivated audiences, to obviate all blemishes of style, of manner, of action, and of speech, blemishes which, of themselves, were both vulgar and grotesque, — when one realises the handicap of early environment that Clara

Morris overcame by sheer histrionic power and conviction, amazement is tinged with mystery. On the stage, Miss Morris never entirely lost the awkwardness and crudeness that her lack of social training had so unfortunately settled upon her; her gestures never ceased to be narrow in range and monotonous in effect; her voice never lost its nasal twang nor its blurring "r;" she never rid herself of her uncultivated enunciation, her rough intonation, and her positively incorrect pronunciation.

What, then, was Clara Morris? Was she actress or phenomenon, artist or exotic? That she had power cannot be disputed. That she afterward lost this power is also a fact. Although Miss Morris has proved by her writings that she possesses intelligence of high order and versatile quality, it is likely that acting with her was mainly instinctive. Of course, she had a method and an art of her own, and they amply sufficed for her purposes while the fire of her genius was blazing with its early fierceness and spontaneity. Neither her method nor her art, however, was complete or fully under her control — else the lamentable

CLARA MORRIS

collapse of both in later years would have been avoided. Art is a permanent possession, wholly apart from personality, as is shown by that wonder-worker, Sarah Bernhardt, also an emotional actress of remarkable temperamental strength, whose power, however, has increased instead of weakening. Never in all her long career did Sarah Bernhardt act Marguerite Gautier in " Camille " with the force, the conviction, and the understanding that she displayed during her visit to the United States in 1901.

The clearest insight into the complexities of Clara Morris's strange emotional and technical equipment has been furnished by her own summing up of her thoughts regarding herself while she was playing, by her account of the stimulus she used in order to reach the necessary point of excited emotionalism, and by her description of the quality of hysteria she was accustomed to provoke for the purpose of affecting her audiences. Miss Morris wrote :

" The same words, of course, become mechanical so far as mere speech goes. I open my mouth and they naturally troop forth ; yet

I feel the part, and, if I did not, my audience would not, either. There must seem to be tears, not only in my eyes but in my voice. In order to obtain the right mood, after the part has become so familiar that the woes of the personage cease to affect me, I am obliged to resort to outside influences; that is, I indulge in the luxury of grief by thinking over somebody else's woes, and, when everything else fails, I think that I am dead, and then I cry for myself! There are, when I am on the stage, three separate currents of thought in my mind: one in which I am keenly alive to Clara Morris, to all the details of the play, to the other actors and how they act, and to the audience; another about the play and the character I represent; and, finally, the thought that really gives me the stimulus for acting. For instance, when I repeat such and such a line, it fits like words to music to this under thought, which may be of some dead friend, of a story of Bret Harte's, of a poem, or maybe even some pathetic scrap from a newspaper. As to really losing one's self in a part, that will not do; it is worse to be too sympathetic than to have too much art. I must cry in my emotional rôles, and feel enough to cry, but I must not allow myself to become so affected as to mumble my words, to redden my nose, or to become hysterical."

In Miss Morris's profound insincerity will be found the explanation of the contradictory fact that she was one of the most "intense" emotional actresses and at the same time one of the worst "guyers" on the stage. Louis James once said that he had played in "Miss Multon" with Clara Morris when her acting had not only her audience but her fellow actors in a condition almost hysterical. In the scene where the heroine flings herself at her husband's feet and exclaims in broken accents, "Maurice, for God's sake, let me see my children!" Mr. James declared that he could not speak for a full minute. He looked at her, and the tears were streaming down her face. Yet in that moment of supreme agony he heard her whisper, "I say, what ails you up there? Are you dumb?" The effect was like a shower bath. This trait of Clara Morris was thoroughly characteristic. In her early days, when she was a member of the Union Square company, it is said that many an actor dreaded to have a scene with her when she was in a mood to "guy," and that she was literally the terror of Charles Thorne's life, although he, too, had something of a reputation for "guying."

"To a great many acute observers," wrote "Nym Crinkle," "she was like a woman with a deep corroding sorrow that is continually hidden by badinage, and that only comes tumultuously to the surface in intense moments of simulation. Education she had none, but she made smartness and intuition take its place, and intelligence bowed to her and beauty envied her. To those of us who tried to look into her heart, she drew down the blinds of her Bohemianism and defied us with murmurs frivol. In the course of time she became wholly an actress. All that once existed in her individuality became invaded by professionalism; she grew to act as she breathed. . . . I could see that this woman protected herself from her own emotions by 'guying' them. She held her phantom consciousness in check till she got before an audience. But she simulated habitually. . . . But this was the most magnetic, the most inscrutable, the most gifted of the actresses of her time. Some of the effects she produced defied analysis, but were acknowledged by everybody. I don't think she ever had a high perception of dramatic art. I never regarded her as an artist at all — only as a natural phenomenon, and in a certain sense a genius peculiar to our country and to our stage. But her sway was irresistible. Salvini himself never produced a finer or more pronounced sensation on the popular nerves than she did."

Although Clara Morris had some reputation in the West as a leading woman before she came to New York, her career really began with her assumption of the part of Anne Sylvester, in Augustin Daly's adaptation of Wilkie Collins's "Man and Wife," at the Fifth Avenue Theatre, New York, on September 13, 1870. James Lewis had recommended Miss Morris to Mr. Daly, and she had been engaged as "walking lady." Agnes Ethel was the popular favourite in New York at that time, and had made a decided success in such parts as Frou Frou and Camille. Being the leading woman of Mr. Daly's company, Anne Sylvester naturally fell to her.

Miss Morris was first cast for the comedy part of Blanche Lundy. She scarcely got it into her hands, however, before Anne Sylvester was substituted for it, Miss Ethel having refused to play the character on moral grounds, and Miss Ione Burke, Miss Ethel's next in rank in the Daly company, being away on her vacation. It has often been erroneously asserted that Fanny Davenport also refused to appear as Anne Sylvester before the part was passed over to Miss Morris. That is not true, however. Fanny Davenport, at that time, was scarcely more than a girl, strong and husky and good-natured, but no actress.

Miss Morris's next notable success was as Cora in " L'Article 47," produced by Mr. Daly on April 2, 1872, her mad scene in this play being regarded as a marvel of realism and dramatic power. Alixe, in Daly's adaptation of " The Comtesse de Somerive," produced on January 23, 1873, showed her in a different light, and as the simple trusting maiden, she reduced the audience, as the character unfolded, to mingled tears and raptures. After her appearance in " Madelein Morel," on May 20, 1873, Miss Morris left the Daly forces, and after a time in the Union Square company, became a star, continuing as such for about twenty years, her notable assumptions being Camille, Miss Multon, and Odette. She also tried Lady Macbeth, Evadne, and Jane Shore, but not successfully, though she did appear to advantage with Tommaso Salvini in " La Morte Civile."

CHAPTER IX.

THE DRAMATISED NOVEL

HE combination of an insistent demand for new plays with a decided unwillingness on the part of managers to risk their money on doubtful ventures was responsible for a curious theatrical phenomenon, which was known as the dramatised novel. The inception of the craze, for it was literally that, dated back to the unusual success of " Trilby," in 1895, and it continued with increasing vigour until the end of the season of 1900–01, when it became gratefully apparent that its popularity was on the wane. The managers, however, who failed to perceive that the vein was worked out, continued to flood the market with undesirable products, offering dramatised novels with a zeal that, devoted to a worthy cause, would have won for them immediate entrance into the hall of theatrical fame.

The dramatisation of the novel is almost as old as the novel itself. Dickens's works in particular were utilised for stage purposes as regularly as they were published. The peculiar thing about the recent enthusiasm along the line of the dramatised novel was found in the perfectly mechanical way in which the transference of the story to the stage was accomplished. There was no selecting nor weighing of merits, no casting up of dramatic possibilities in the story under consideration. Every bit of fiction, no matter how ephemeral, that sold enough copies to attract a trifle more than passing attention, was seized by the manager, who had to have a play but who lacked the judgment and the courage to pick one out and produce it, and rushed upon the stage with celerity that was indeed astonishing. The natural product of the curious craze was the quick leap into the ranks of the dramatists of a class of men, most of them stage-managers by profession, who made a specialty of dramatising novels, and who would guarantee out of hand to dramatise anything from a census report to the latest edition of Noah Webster's dictionary. One of the most prolific of the group was Edward E. Rose, who was ready to turn out something that would act from any sort of material whatsoever. Whether the resulting play would contain anything in the least resembling the novel, of which it was supposed to be a stage version, was entirely another question, and one about which Mr. Rose was wise enough never to trouble himself.

"ALICE OF OLD VINCENNES"

A fair specimen of Mr. Rose's style was "Alice of Old Vincennes," derived in Mr. Rose's unprejudiced fashion from Maurice Thompson's novel of that name, and starred in by Virginia Harned during the season of 1901–02. Two things were necessary to a proper enjoyment of Mr. Rose's play: first and most important, never to have read Mr. Thompson's novel; second, an extremely vivid and elastic imagination. Thus equipped, one could endure the ordeal with reasonable composure. In dramatic form "Alice of Old Vincennes" was a four-act melodrama of colourful nature. It displayed uniforms of British red, worn by all the villains in the action, like-

VIRGINIA HARNED
As Alice in " Alice of Old Vincennes "

wise uniforms of Continental blue and buff, garbing the stalwart hero and his equally stalwart comrades. Moreover, to augment the James Fenimore Cooper atmosphere, there were frequent glimpses of leather trousers, of befringed leather shirts, and of coonskin caps, which crowned the heads of our woodsmen forefathers.

The playbill kindly advanced the information that the action passed in the Indiana town of Vincennes and was concerned with the Revolutionary War, but, as far as essentials went, it might all have happened in South Africa during the recent British disturbance with the Boers. The action, however, had one definite object in view, and that was to bring Alice and the British Colonel Hamilton together on the stage for a strenuous struggle in full view of the audience. Hamilton was, of course, the villain, otherwise there would have been no interest in the fight. This is how Mr. Rose arranged it: Colonel Clark's forces have surrounded Vincennes and are ready to attack the British garrison on a signal, which is to be the firing of a pistol from the fort. To Beverley, Alice's lover, is assigned the hazardous duty of penetrating the fort and selecting the proper moment for giving the signal. Beverley gets to the fort, but is discovered there and imprisoned, and the chances for signalling the American forces seem slim indeed. However, nothing is impossible to the dramatiser of a novel.

Beverley having been tucked away out of sight, Alice and Hamilton are alone on the stage, he pressing his attentions on her, she resisting. He becomes more ardent and tries to embrace her, but she snatches a pistol from his belt and holds him at bay. But the signal! It must be given! There is but a single charge in the weapon! If she fire out of the window, Clark, to be sure, will hear, but that will leave her unarmed at the mercy of Hamilton. If she shoot Hamilton inside the building, Clark will not hear the signal. Evidently the intrepid young woman never considered the possibility of first shooting Hamilton wherever it appeared to be most convenient, then reloading the weapon and firing it off outside the window for the benefit of Colonel Clark.

However, Alice did not hesitate in the choice between country and honour. She fired out of the window for Clark's benefit, and then, when Hamilton rushed upon her, seized a trusty sword that happened to be handy and defended herself so lustily that the gallant Hamilton was willing enough to retire from the contest even before the Continental troops captured the fort. It may be added that while one cannot extol the literary quality of Mr. Rose's work high above the heavens, he can at least declare with measured enthusiasm that Mr. Rose knows his school of stage-craft thoroughly. The mechanical certainty of his theatricalism is not to be denied.

"BEAUCAIRE"

A dramatisation of superior quality to "Alice of Old Vincennes" was Mrs. Evelyn Greenleaf Sutherland's five-act comedy made from Booth Tarkington's charming novelette, "Monsieur Beaucaire." Mrs. Sutherland's play was called "Beaucaire," and it provided an acceptable vehicle for Richard Mansfield during the season of 1901–02. Notwithstanding that it was derived from a novel, "Beaucaire" was a whole play, entirely capable of meeting criticism on its own merits, a thoroughly charming light comedy, clean and neat in construction, witty, entertaining, and dramatic; a trifle, if one choose to look at it with ponderous eyes, but an interesting frame for the exhibition of an interesting character, which shone brightly against a romantic and picturesque background.

" Beaucaire " excelled for a number of well defined reasons. It told a vivid, interesting, and slightly original story in a convincing way; it presented, with due attention to detail and illusion, pleasing pictures of manners and customs fascinatingly strange and, incidentally, historically edifying; it added to these a naïve, but on the whole attractive, flow of wit and fancy that was quite exhilarating; but, more than all else, it brought into being a personage, magnetically mystifying, ideally chivalrous, inspiringly courageous, a perfect lover, a hearty friend, and a generous enemy, — in short, the paragon of all that was noble, honourable, and admirable, and, in spite of his virtues, no wretched lay figure stuffed for a mummer's ranting, but a splendid conception of a man.

This Beaucaire was a delight. One envied Mr. Mansfield the rare pleasure of impersonating him. The actor, moreover, succeeded in meeting the character fully half-way. He completed what the originator had begun. Mr. Tarkington made Beaucaire real to the imagination. Mr. Mansfield substituted for the phantom figure of the printed page the physical reality of the stage, transforming the dream Beaucaire into a Beaucaire of flesh and blood, heart and individuality. Thus Mr. Mansfield again illustrated his mastery of subtle character delineation and of eccentric light comedy acting. Again he exhibited his art in its most delicate and delightful form, forming in Beaucaire a character that at once took place beside the debonair Prince Karl and the exquisite Beau Brummel. In fact, Beaucaire was something of a union of the two, the joining of Prince Karl's sweet sentiment and perfect chivalry to Brummel's keen intelligence and fine courage. Even as were both Prince Karl and Beau Brummel, so also was Beaucaire — the full-length portrait of a true gentleman.

"WHEN KNIGHTHOOD WAS IN FLOWER"

Paul Kester was responsible for the stage version of Charles Major's novel, "When

Knighthood Was in Flower," which was exploited for the benefit of Julia Marlowe, and which proved attractive enough to keep that actress in New York through the entire season of 1900–01. There is no question, however, that the main portion of this attractiveness centred in Miss Marlowe, who acted the contrary Mary Tudor, a personage more or less historic. Not that the antique Mary counted for much — at least, not after the cool indifference of a formal introduction. It was Julia Marlowe that the people paid their good money to see, Julia Marlowe shrewish and Julia Marlowe tender and loving; Julia Marlowe vixenish and raging, and Julia Marlowe so soft and wooingly feminine that the heart melted in very sympathy; Julia Marlowe inconsistently womanish in doublet and hose and Julia Marlowe bold and fearless in her proper petticoats, defying monarch on his throne and peasant in his hovel, all for the sake of the man whom she loved. Who so adamant to the sweet and soothing influence of winsome personality that he could resist or would resist the potency of the appeal?

Still, there was something to be said on the

JULIA MARLOWE
As Mary Tudor in " When Knighthood Was in Flower "

side of Mr. Kester's play. It was actually a dramatisation in the particular that it followed with reasonable accuracy the trend of Mr. Major's plot and gave the auditor in the theatre an excellent idea of the story that Mr. Major had to tell. It also reproduced with fair likeness Mr. Major's conceptions of his characters, with the added garnish, of course, that seems to be unavoidable in transferal from book to playhouse. In this particular, the hero, Charles Brandon, was the worst sufferer, for he came forth from Mr. Kester's treatment robbed of all distinction, simply the ordinary, invincible hero of romantic melodrama. With Henry VIII., the dramatist was much more successful, preserving in the Falstaffian king a thoroughly interesting and entertaining individual. Otherwise, however, with the exception of the Princess Mary, the personages in the drama inclined toward the colourless — or say rather, they were mere sketches in outline, lacking detail and finish.

Doubtless, if one were disposed to probe far beneath the surface impression of Mr. Kester's play, if he were to judge the work according to an adequate art standard, there would be revealed faults plenty and to spare. However, such faults as there were could be generally summed up under the heading of inexperience. "When Knighthood Was in Flower" showed plainly that Mr. Kester had not mastered fully the mechanics of his trade. This did not deny him imagination, or inherent force, or appreciation of the dramatic in situation and character, but it did declare that he had not learned how to present his situations, characters, and climaxes, so that they would strike the audience with the acme of dramatic and theatrical effect. Although he did not work up his complex situations to the fulness of their power, in the handling of a simple and natural episode, where the stress was more honestly emotional and less mechanically necessary, Mr. Kester manifested both directness and force. For this reason his third act in "When Knighthood Was in Flower" was the best one in the play.

By the time this act is reached, Mary's love for Charles has been fully exploited; we have heard the king declare that she must marry Louis of France; we have witnessed her flight in male attire with Charles. Now the two have arrived at Bristol. At the Bow and String Tavern they meet the ship's company, with which they expect to sail for New Spain. All seems to be going finely, when King Henry and his guards come suddenly upon them. In a twinkling Charles is a prisoner and Mary as good as the bride of France. With his hero and his heroine in this plight, Mr. Kester unexpectedly quit melodrama and gave for the moment a sincere and convincing presentation of a scene emotionally strong. Mary's plea for her lover's life, her promise to wed Louis if only Charles be given his freedom, the parting of the couple, — all these happenings, one quickly following the other, were genuinely touching. They were also beautifully acted by Miss Marlowe, who found therein golden opportunity to display the simplicity and truth of her art at its best.

" DAVID HARUM "

Of all the long list of dramatised novels, none achieved greater popularity nor provided more rich enjoyment than " David Harum," as made into a play from Edward Noyes Westcott's unique work by R. and M. W. Hitchcock (with the aid, so it was said, of the versatile Mr. Rose), and as played with William H. Crane in the title part. The play "David Harum" was a solid rural drama, and as far as David himself was concerned it was satisfactory to an exceptional degree. Inasmuch as David was practically the whole show, there was so little left with which to find fault that one felt no need of fussing about it. Every one of the country characters was excellently well done, and it was a pity that the city folks, of whom fortunately there were only three, could not have been treated equally as well. Not one of them, however, had an iota of humanity in him, and the love story in which they were concerned was literally spoon victuals.

Further than to extol its character studies of country types, there is no call for undue enthusiasm regarding the play. It might justly be said that the whole was saved by its parts. There were bits that ranged high as comedy — one of the best the horse trade with the deacon; there were other bits that were brilliantly farcical — notably the effective tableau of the deacon in the thunder-storm belabouring with might and main the obsti-

WILLIAM H. CRANE
As David Harum

nate horse that would stand without hitching. Mr. Crane's portrayal of David Harum was one of the few instances where a pronouncedly effective book character has been transferred to the stage in a manner entirely satisfactory to the reader's etherealised notion of what the character should be. William Gillette's Sherlock Holmes was another instance. David Harum suited Mr. Crane perfectly, and in it he hid his own personality most surprisingly. Moreover, he succeeded in being pathetic without a hint of mawkishness, something that only rarely had he previously accomplished.

"BESIDE THE BONNIE BRIER BUSH"

The dramatisation of Ian MacLaren's Scotch tale, "Beside the Bonnie Brier Bush," was done by Tom Hall and James MacArthur, who brought forth from the struggle a none too strenuous melodrama, with little originality either of plot or development, but of decided popular flavour in the matter of sentiment and of much real interest in several of its characters. As the hard old Scot, J. H. Stoddart, who starred in the play, was provided with a part well suited to his peculiar histrionic style and equipment. Such as found Doctor Watson's book something to weep over in lachrymose enjoyment were probably a trifle shocked at the crude treatment accorded the reverend gentleman's pretty reminiscences, sentimental musings, and idealistic speculations; but crudeness usually does result from the attempt to translate readable sentiment into actable drama. One can be idealistic about nothing to his heart's content in a book, but he must be definite in the theatre, where there is neither time nor opportunity to speculate. In the theatre one must either tell a story or study a character.

The greater part of the play " Beside the Bonnie Brier Bush " was given over to the telling of a story, derived, I imagine, from all the books that Doctor Watson ever wrote. In the first act, one found Lord Kilspindle's son, Lord Donald Hay, making love to Flora Campbell and then wedding her by what turned out to be a valid Scotch marriage. In the second act, Flora's father, not understanding the wedding part, was seen to drive his daughter from the house and blot her name from the family Bible. In the third act, Lachlan Campbell's repentance was shown, as well as Flora's return to succour afforded her by the sympathetic neighbours. In the last act, the various love matches were straightened out, — that between Annie and Thomas, and that between Kate Carnegie and the minister, — the curtain falling after Lord Hay had declared that Flora was his wife, being corroborated in his statement by "Posty," who witnessed from behind a haystack the secret compact that made a marriage according to the Scotch law.

Besides being thus commonplace in story, the play was plentifully besprinkled with weeps, heavily freighted with theatricalism, and thickly punctuated with grandiloquent catch phrases that angled persuasively for applause. But it did have some good characters, among them two of exceptionally effective low comedy — Archibald McKittrick, the "Posty," and William McLure, the shrewd, old-style doctor. Of similar excellence, though of minor importance, were the dairy maid, Annie, and her shepherd lover, Thomas.

Lachlan Campbell, as a dramatic character, suffered in effectiveness through the exaggeration of its leading element, parental sternness.

Campbell's unmitigated brutality in barring the door against his daughter placed him so wholly in the wrong, made him so evident an example of pig-headed bigotry and intense selfishness, that any sympathy at all with his father's grief over what he believed to be his daughter's disgrace was entirely out of the question. There may be fathers like that in Scotland, but not many folks here have any knowledge of them outside of melodrama. Mr. Stoddart acted the part robustly, vigorously, and vividly, with full exposition of every situation and with great elaboration of every detail. While he may have been justified by his text in not softening his sternness into something approaching humanity, and while his persistent hardness may have increased the theatrical effect, it is also quite certain that it completely destroyed all possible sympathetic appeal.

CHAPTER X.

ONE of the few modern Continental dramas that has secured a position of some stability in the theatre in the United States is Hermann Sudermann's play of German provincial life, " Heimat," or " Magda," as the English version is called. This drama has been given in its native German by Heinrich Conried's company in the Irving Place Theatre, New York, in French by Sarah Bernhardt, in Italian by Eleanora Duse, and in English by Helena Modjeska and Mrs. Patrick Campbell. Mrs. Campbell appeared as Magda on the occasion of her first tour in this country during the season of 1901–1902. It proved to be by far the most notable of her impersonations.

Seeing this play acted, one's attention is immediately attracted to a peculiarity in Sudermann's construction, which makes an audience, however interested and thrilled, seem to be cold and lacking in enthusiasm. Sudermann has a knack of forcing his most startling climaxes into the middle of his acts. There one does not like to applaud, because he does not wish to interrupt or retard the dramatic action. These middle-act climaxes being thus past without any marked outward manifestation of appreciation, Sudermann starts in on a new development, and then drops his curtain just when the suspense is beginning, but before there is really anything to applaud.

What grows especially on one, the more familiar he becomes with Sudermann's " Magda," is the hopelessness of Lieutenant-Colonel Schwartze. At first, when the drama was new, there seemed to be, to one who fancied that he had some notion of the provincial German's strange and perverted idea of honour, sufficient excuse for the pig-headedness of Magda's father to permit one to bestow on him the atom of sympathy that was necessary in order to bring the character within the range of possibility. Upon further acquaintance with the facts of the case, however, every vestige of sympathy vanished, and old

MRS. PATRICK CAMPBELL
As Magda

Schwartze stood forth a selfish, obstinate, unreasonable, and inhuman brute, who deserved to die, if ever any one deserved to die. Undoubtedly Mrs. Campbell's human Magda, as contrasted with Mr. G. S. Titheradge's exceedingly blunt and unsoftened Schwartze, helped in their presentation of the play to emphasise this condition of things. Still, I am convinced that the condition is really inherent, though it may sometimes be tucked partially out of sight by less pronounced acting. In fact, wholly to eliminate it would be to ruin the motive and purpose of the drama.

The evidence in the case bears out this theory. Schwartze, it will be remembered, was guilty of the first error. His daughter refused to marry the minister, and he drove her from his house, — a punishment altogether out of proportion to the fault, if fault it actually was. Eleven years passed without his especially troubling himself about her. He did not know, indeed, whether she was alive or dead. At the end of that time, however, she unfortunately yielded to a sentimental weakness — it was scarcely more than that, though coupled with it was a lingering affection for her younger sister. She accepted an invitation to sing in her native town, reëntered her father's house, succumbed again to sentiment as against her better judgment, and consented to stay there for the time being.

The moment that this outcast daughter once more came under his roof, the father usurped the authority that eleven years before he had violently and cruelly relinquished; and he presumed to question this woman, whom he had forced unprotected into the street, regarding her conduct during the period of her freedom. He attempted to order her present and future life according to his own narrow and conventional code of righteousness and morality. Naturally his will was steadfastly opposed; it was right that it should be opposed. Magda had sinned, but she had expiated her sin with tears and toil and achievement; she had striven and risen far above her old self; she was in every sense a strong, upright, and noble woman. Schwartze, too, had sinned, equally with his daughter — even more so, for he was directly responsible for her sin; but he had not expiated his sin. He had indeed suffered, but his suffering had not brought him to a realisation of his own fault. His suffering he blamed upon another; his sin he cherished, and he continued to cherish it, until in the end it killed him.

That is Sudermann's play, and it is an absolutely logical working out of the problem involved. The ethics throughout are positive and true. Yet the result is not wholly satisfactory. One still hunts for a solution to a problem, for which there is no solution, except the gradual one that comes with the living of an honest, sincere, and upright life. Magda summed up the situation in its entirety with this agonising question, "Why did I ever come back?" Magda, by her dreadful experience, again proved it impossible — even as every one, who has tried it, has time after time proved it impossible — to live under restrictions or amid conditions that have been outgrown. "Why did I ever come back?" The wise man never does come back.

As already stated, Mrs. Campbell presented a human Magda. Indeed, humanity appeared to be the vital and moving quality in all of this actress's work. Although not a player of wide range or versatility, her acting did possess ease, authority, and spontaneity, and especially that realistic and deceptive quality, which made it difficult to separate the individuality of the player from the individuality of the part.　She proved a superior delineator of character; she got at the woman.　But she was not in the least an impersonator; she fitted every part to herself, either not being able, or else not trying, to distinguish them from herself or from each other by the aid of external peculiarities.　Thus when Paula Tanqueray was coarse, one instantly received the impression that Mrs. Campbell herself was coarse; and when Magda Schwartze burst into a fury at the sleek Von Keller, one forthwith imagined that Mrs. Campbell was accustomed to burst into just such furies.　Of course, it by no means followed that the actress, in her own person, would do any of those things, or that she expressed contempt with an odd little sniff, or recklessness with a hard half-laugh, or shrugged her shoulders when she was emotionally excited.　It simply meant that Mrs. Campbell fixed these and other ways — they were not absolutely mannerisms, though they might grow to be mannerisms, if not watched closely

—on all her characters, and fixed them so solidly that they seemed to be a part of herself.

Because she did this, and because she trimmed her characters to her own personality instead of trimming her personality to her characters, Mrs. Campbell could not be called an impersonator.   But although not an impersonator, an actor may still be a striking and vivid, a realistic and comprehensive, delineator of character, and such I believe Mrs. Campbell to be. Moreover, she seemed an actress with an exceptionally fine instinct for effect, a quality that was particularly prominent in her Magda.   Her first entrance in this character, as she advanced from the open door at the back of the stage with outstretched arms to meet her sister, instantly etched itself on the memory. It was like a flashlight in its effect.   Added to these impressive qualities in Mrs. Campbell's technical equipment, was her voice, perhaps singly the most potent of the various elements that combined to make her an interesting study.   With every actor it is the voice, almost the voice alone, that conveys sincerity and forces conviction.   Mrs. Campbell's voice was supercharged with emotion. Speaking, it compelled attention, won sympathy, engendered emotion, expressed ably the shades of love and tenderness as well as the harshness of scorn and contempt.

"PELLEAS AND MELISANDE"

To Mrs. Campbell we were indebted for the first presentation in this country of one of Maurice Maeterlinck's curious dramas. The play was "Pelleas and Melisande," nominated in the bond a "tragical romance." With the drama was given Gabriel Faure's music, the two forming an interesting exposition of the relative effectiveness in the realm of the purely imaginative of the art of music and of drama. Considering that Maeterlinck's attempt was to make a play that should mean nothing in itself, but should suggest a multitude of meanings to the imagination, it was not altogether strange that the musician was more successful in formulating the dramatist's ideal than was the dramatist himself. The musician, through the medium of sound, approximately accomplished what the dramatist was unable to do through the medium of words and actions, declared by flesh and blood men and women. The musician made an emotional suggestion, vivid and real, and at the same time retaining all its idealism and intangibility. There was romance in the music, the romance of the land of Nowhere, with its sighings and its moanings, its love that is passionate and pure, its laughter that is hollow and mocking.

But one cannot do that sort of thing on the stage. One must have reality there — reality to go with the very real human beings that act on the stage, reality of emotion, positive, understandable, instantaneous, to make one forget that the rooms of the castle are only painted and that the forests are merely canvas stretched on wooden frames. When one gets a poetical impression from the stage, it is the result of the perfect expression of sincere emotion in beautiful, living, impressionable words. J. W. Mackall's translation of Maeterlinck's play did not have that inspired quality. What mysticism, romance, imagination, or suggestion could one get from such thoroughly ordinary phrases as "follow my advice" and "take anybody with you"? Poetry has a language of its own, and that language is the only one appropriate to poetry. As for the characteristically Maeterlinck repetition of words and sentences, like all artificialities, it served no valid purpose on the stage. The effect produced was not emphatic — only monotonous and slightly ludicrous.

The story of the play was a retelling of the "Francesca da Rimini" tale, with place, time, and even characters made purposely indefinite and undetermined. Melisande, the woman in the case, was an innocent child, whom the somewhat elderly Golaud found weeping beside a pool in a wood. "Come with me," he said to her. "Where are you going?" she asked. "I do not know," he answered. "I, too, am lost." So they went away together and were married. Next Melisande and her brother-in-law, Pelleas, were discovered together beside the Fountain of the Blind. Melisande, who had been carelessly toying with the ring that her husband gave her, lost it in the water. "What shall I do? What shall I do?" she cried. "Tell the truth," wisely counselled Pelleas.

She did not follow the advice, however. She lied to Golaud and talked about a cave where the ring was, until Golaud embarrassed her by sending her to this cave to find it. It was night, and Pelleas accompanied her, willing enough by that time to help in the deception. Asleep in the cave were three old men, and so the couple did not enter. No more was heard of the ring, but there followed in the next scene a sort of Romeo and Juliet balcony scene between Pelleas and Melisande, during which he made love to her long black hair and got caught at it by his brother. Notwithstanding that, Pelleas and Melisande again met at the Fountain of the Blind, and their love-making at that meeting provided what was far and away the best acting scene in the play. The childlike innocence of Melisande was remarkably well indicated, and even Pelleas's reprehensible behaviour seemed for the moment compatible with nobility of nature. But once more the husband came upon the lovers. He killed Pelleas, and then rushed after Melisande, who discreetly fled toward the castle. Judging by the talk of a mysterious body of servants, who occupied the stage at the opening of the last act, he caught her. The wound which he inflicted upon her was scarcely more than a pin-prick,—so the doctor said,—but it sufficed, and she died.

Of course, it was all symbolic of something —pool in the wood, Fountain of the Blind, ring that was lost, cave by the seas, even the strange group of mumbling, chattering servants; but to ascertain what it meant, one did not feel any intense, uncontrollable desire to search either very far or very diligently. No man with a hot, burning, imperious message would make such hard work of imparting it as did Maeterlinck of his message in this play; and it is a question whether any message which is not hot, burning, and imperious is worth listening to. The man with something vital to say says it right out loud so that he can be heard and understood. He is the man who is listened to, and usually he is the only man who should be listened to. As far as the acting was concerned, there was commendation for Mrs. Campbell's remarkable instinct for the picturesquely effective. It served to vitalise her Melisande and to make the poor creature at least interesting to the eye. Genuine emotional power in the presentation was impossible, however, not only in Melisande, but in all the other characters, for there was no groundwork of truth, of sincerity, or of reality on which to build.

CHAPTER XI

HENRY IRVING IN MELODRAMA

ENRY IRVING'S first great success in London, the success that placed him in the way of attaining the eminence that has brought him general recognition as the leading English actor of his time, was his Mathias in " The Bells," a weird and distinctly melodramatic conception ; and since that time some of his most remarkable work has been done in melodrama. Under that category would come his spectacular assumption of the dual parts in " The Lyons Mail," his eccentric character study in " Louis XI.," his interesting Napoleon in " Madame Sans Gêne," and his Robespierre. In fact, from first to last, it is likely that fully two-thirds of the impersonations on which are builded Henry Irving's name and fame are thoroughly melodramatic.

HENRY IRVING
As Mathias in " The Bells."

In "The Lyons Mail," made by Charles Reade from the French of Moreau, Girardin, and Delacour, Mr. Irving plays Joseph Lesurques, an honourable merchant of Paris, and Dubosc, a highwayman and robber. The complications of the play arise from the fact that physically the two men so closely resemble one another, that the innocent Lesurques is arrested, condemned, and nearly guillotined for a crime committed by Dubosc. Although it is of itself a melodrama of the finer sort, the life of " The Lyons Mail " has been prolonged, not because of its especial merit, but because of the wonderfully vivid, intensely realistic, and marvellously differentiated acting of Mr. Irving as Lesurques and Dubosc.

When a skilful pianist sits down before his instrument and dashes off a lot of scales and arpeggios, one may be amazed at his digital dexterity, but one does not call the resultant sounds music. At the best, the player has produced nothing more elevated than refined and classified noise. Ordinarily, the presentation of a dual rôle by an actor is analogous to that sort of piano playing. The actor's technique may be astonishing, but the product of his technique usually is not, in the highest sense, art, any more than the many faces of the lightning change "artist" in the varieties are art. In fact, the conventional actor of a dual rôle and the "man of many faces" in the variety theatre are on precisely the same plane. Each is an exceptional sort of a gymnast, who garbs himself externally with astonishing rapidity and sometimes with mystifying results, but who does not change the individuality of his various personages in the slightest degree. From first to last there is in evidence always the same man, arrayed in different cut of clothes and sporting constantly changing designs in whiskers.

The severest possible test that could be made of an actor playing two different characters would be to compel him to declare the two different individualities without changing at all the clothes that the two men wear. It was not exactly that test to which Mr. Irving submitted in "The Lyons Mail," but it was a test at least approximate to it. He did make manifest, without a suspicion or a chance of ambiguity, the individualities of Lesurques and Dubosc without adding or subtracting a line of facial make-up; and as for clothes, he limited himself to swapping a short coat for a long one and a good hat for a battered one.

Mr. Irving's acting of this dual rôle was art, for the reason that he presented in one play, not two different representations of a single character, but two wholly dissimilar men, who, nevertheless, in face and figure — in everything except expression and identity — were the same man. Mr. Irving created out of one body two separate and antagonistic personages, and he did it so well and so thoroughly that his Lesurques and Dubosc have kept " The Lyons Mail " in the theatre all these years. Lively dodging on and off the stage, rapid putting on and taking off of garments, all the theatricalism in the world could never have done so much. Both this Lesurques and Dubosc showed Mr. Irving to be a remarkable character actor, and they also plainly declared where his genius was and where his talent was. The brutal, drunken, degenerate Dubosc was the inspiration of decided genius in the interpretation of eccentric character types.

Lesurques, except possibly the Lesurques of those quiet, pathos-weighted moments of the second act, when fearfulness of the future was fairly dawning, was the work of the talented player.

"LOUIS XI."

To know Mr. Irving at his best in a character part, one should see his impersonation of Louis XI. in Dion Boucicault's adaptation of Cassimer DeLavigne's play. This part is both pictorial and intellectual. In its outward aspects it demands the representation of the physical decay of advancing age. Lined in the face, glinting from the eyes, evidenced in the walk, in the nervous movements of the hands, in the suspicious and fearsome poise of the head is the burden of senility, made still more burdensome by the gnawing of unconquerable dread of the future, of impotent fear of the present, and of unrepentant remorse for the past. There had to be uncovered, as well, the source of all these visual effects, the mind, with its noisomeness of deceit, of avarice, and of rank hypocrisy. Without this, the outward seeming would have been not only repulsive but inexplicable as

well. In fact, the far greater task of the actor
came in adequately conveying the mentality of
this King of France. Although as a composite
the character appeared to be complex, the
actor had to make plain its underlying simplicity — to show how fear and selfishness were
the motives for every action. By means of a
variety of detail, compiled and arranged with
due regard for perspective and proportion, the
actor was obliged so to order and arrange
the infinite and indefinite little things that,
in the collocation necessarily made therefrom
by the spectator, they formed one definite big
thing.

Mr. Irving's great achievement was in
making his Louis easily understood; one
perceived the bearing of the character at once,
and classified it correctly at first sight. In
Louis XI. was portrayed an advanced form of
moral idiocy. Selfishness had so worked into
the fibre of the king's being that he had literally lost all ability to distinguish between right
and wrong. His haunting fear and his constant terror and dread were of death; and yet,
even in the hour of his dissolution, he could
not refrain from craft and deceit. He had lost

the ability to be honest, and this loss was a tragedy far more terrible than any conceivable death. Playing this part, Mr. Irving displayed to the greatest possible advantage the peculiar artistic gifts that make him preëminent and unapproachably great in eccentric character impersonations. Give Mr. Irving a man set apart from his fellows by some uncommon twist, either of physique or of mentality, or, as is usually the case, of both, and he will picture this man on the stage with a force and a concentrated power, a picturesqueness and a wealth of detail, not to be excelled. With keenness of conception and exact accentuation of the abnormal qualities of mind, he unites vividness and vigour of histrionic effect. In no other one part, unless it be that vital bit of creation, the old soldier in " Waterloo," does Mr. Irving show his genius for character acting so advantageously as he does in " Louis XI."

" MADAME SANS GÊNE "

" Madame Sans Gêne," by Emile Moreau and Victorien Sardou, was more of a vehicle for Miss Ellen Terry than it was for Mr. Irving. Napoleon, as pictured in the play, is an amusing personage, and, perhaps, an historically correct personage as well; but he is disappointing, none the less. Napoleon had his full share of littleness, it is true, but that fact did not prevent him from being a full-grown hero. It does go against the grain to see him depicted only as a household tyrant and a yelping slave to petty and unworthy jealousy. Of course, this feeling of resentment is entirely prejudicial and absolutely indefensible. Neither Sardou nor Moreau asked my advice regarding the sort of Napoleon they should portray, and I do not suppose that at this late day they are especially interested in what I think of the matter. Their portrayal of Napoleon is amusing, and amusing is doubtless exactly what they intended that it should be.

The chief figure in " Madame Sans Gêne " is not Napoleon, however, but the buxom washerwoman, Catherine, as whom Miss Terry practically starred it during the prologue and three acts of the play, for Catherine is a comedy part, furnishing rare opportunities to the actress who has the personality and the art to make use of them. In no one part, it seemed to me, except her delightful impersonation of Nance Oldfield, has Miss Terry in recent years so deliciously displayed her bubbling, free, and whole-souled merriment. It will be understood that the Sans Gêne acted by Miss Terry was hardly the one imagined by the authors of the play. They had in mind a husky female, coarse-grained and rough-mannered, to whom the title " fishwife," with all the profuseness of profane and obscene talking that the name implies, was literally applicable. The Sardou-Moreau Sans Gêne had just three points in her favour, — her good heart, her sound morals, and her ready wit. In all other respects she was hopeless.

The Terry Sans Gêne was not that sort at all. Her language, it is true, was not precisely classic, and the wiles of the diplomat were far from her. Nor was she skilled in courtly manners or in fine points of etiquette. She was not refined nor cultured; yet she was not vulgar. It is rather delicate work to draw a line between the absence of the superficial polish of society and the presence of native fine feeling and instinct for politeness. Miss Terry did draw such a line, and her success in that particular raised the character of Catherine to a plane distinctly higher than that accorded it by the two dramatists who originally conceived the part. Miss Terry portrayed a woman who was crude socially, awkward and ill at ease amid artificiality, but a woman who was without a taint of vulgarity or even unladylikeness, to use an old-fashioned expression. Her Madame Sans Gêne was independent, but she fought with a rapier, and did not slash with a butcher's cleaver. Miss Terry's acting was rich in detail, well-nigh perfect in its spontaneity, and splendidly positive in its effect. It was full of spirit and of natural and seemingly impromptu humour. There was always simplicity and directness, almost naïveté of method. Still, no points were lost, and such moments of dramatic force as there were received their full expression.

Mr. Irving's Napoleon was a great surprise. When one considers the tall, spare figure, and the thin, sharp-featured face of the English actor, and compares them with the short, plump-bodied, and full-cheeked Napoleon, he is likely to declare that for Mr. Irving so much as even to suggest pictorially the little Corsican would be an impossibility. The secrets of the make-up box are multitudinous, and the results on the human figure of judicious padding are mystifying. Mr. Irving certainly did get himself up so that he presented a fairly recognisable portraiture of the Emperor; and, moreover, he toddled about the stage with jerky, nervous steps, that carried with them not a hint of the Irving walk.

" ROBESPIERRE "

Mr. Irving originally produced "Robespierre" at the Lyceum Theatre, London, on April 15, 1899, and it was first acted in this country in New York, on October 30 following. The drama was written in French, by Sardou, on an order from Mr. Irving, though the dramatist was obliged to formulate his leading character without any personal knowledge of the player whom he was commissioned to fit, for Sardou had never seen Mr. Irving act. The play was translated into English by Laurence Irving. With one exception, "Robespierre" was presented exactly as Sardou wrote it. Sardou's last scene was cut in the Irving production in order to bring the drama within the time limit, and by this cut historical fact was directly violated. In the play as given by Mr. Irving, the suicide of Robespierre was made to occur at the end of the exciting sitting of the Convention in which the Incorruptible, as Robespierre was called, learned that his days of dictatorship were numbered. As a matter of fact, Robespierre's suicide came much later. Arrested in the Convention, Robespierre was confined in the prison of the Luxembourg. Rescued by his friends, he took refuge in the Hôtel de Ville, and it was there that the concluding scene of the Sardou drama was originally laid. Surrounded by his partisans, Robespierre was inclined to take their advice and summon the Communists to rise in opposition to the Convention. He had, in fact, written a proclamation and was about to sign it, when the troops of the Convention made their entry. Robespierre's adherents fled for their lives, and Robespierre, perceiving that his cause was lost, shot himself.

According to Sardou, there still exists an interesting relic of this dramatic scene, which the dramatist portrayed but which has never been acted on the stage, although it has been incorporated in the novel that Angé Galdemar made from the play. The proclamation, which Robespierre had prepared for issuance, was preserved, so Sardou claimed. It contains Robespierre's appeal to the Commune, and at the bottom, in his handwriting, the first two letters of his signature, which he did not have time to finish inscribing. On the paper also is a smear of blood, which might be taken for the flourish of the signature, but which is, in all probability, the blood of Robespierre himself.

From Victorien Sardou, acknowledged past master in the creation of stage effects, one looks for a play thrilling, intense, and vivid; a play cunningly constructed theatrically; a play that often cruelly and brutally, by means of a thousand and one tricks of suspense, contrast, and pictorial device, rends and tears the emotions of the susceptible and unsophisticated; a play that, after all is said, is without heart or substance or convincing motive; a play in which character is a mere external instead of an essential growth and development from the action; a play which moves, not by the irresistible force of its inherent truth, but by the mechanical will of the skilful machinist.

" Robespierre " was a typical Sardou play, and, considered on its proper plane of frank melodrama, was a successful effort. Its eight scenes were pictorially entertaining; its varied episodes, even when they hovered dangerously near the ridiculous, as was the case with the ghost scene of the fourth act, always invited the catch in the breath and the involuntary spread of excitement that is the reward of melodramatic pleading; its characters, too, partook of the same picturesque quality that was evident in the play. The central figure, Robespierre himself, was, in fact, more than merely a part of a picture; he was the one force that kept the action, at times so detached and fragmentary as to threaten disintegration, in any sense a unit.

Most of all, however, this Sardou drama relied for its interest on the always fascinating period of the French Revolution, a period to which Sardou has often had recourse and with the superficialities of which at least he is thoroughly familiar, a period that lends itself with perfect ease to Sardou's graphic and scenic stage productions. With sure theatrical instinct, Sardou seized upon Robespierre, the personification of the Reign of Terror, and made him the central figure of his melodrama. To give the monster of iniquity a passing semblance to humanity, the dramatist invented a youthful love and a son. Robespierre was introduced at the moment when his career had passed its climax. He was seen with his influence waning and his boundless ambition still ungratified. He was represented as vain, cowardly, madly wild in his social imaginings. We followed him through the hypocritical triumphs of his fête of the Supreme Being, and we were with him when he suffered the keen pangs of unrequited parental affection, the fear of doomed death for his son, the terrors of the guilty conscience feeding on remorse, and finally the complete despair of disappointed hopes and vanished authority.

Such was the Robespierre indicated by Sardou and portrayed by Mr. Irving, the character from which the play received its name, and the only character in the play that was to any degree whatsoever developed, the only presence that prevented the drama

HENRY IRVING

from being merely a series of disconnected episodes.

In this connection, it will be interesting to note how few and how small a part of the eight scenes, which comprised the five acts of "Robespierre," had anything to do with advancing the plot. According to Sardou's story, nineteen years before the action began, Robespierre had had a liaison with Clarise de Malucon, who had borne him a son, Olivier. At the opening of the play, Clarise, unknown to Robespierre, is living in seclusion with her son and Marie Therese, her niece, in a cottage in the forest of Montmorency. By an unfortunate chance, she and her niece fall under Robespierre's suspicion and are thrown into prison. The son, crazy with grief and rage, publicly denounces the tyrant and is also imprisoned. Robespierre, however, learns who these, his latest victims, are, and releases Clarise and Marie; but through the machinations of his enemies he loses track of Olivier. Olivier, in the meanwhile, has been set free by the Committee of Public Safety; and unaware of the relationship that Robespierre bears to him, he is bent on assassinating his father. Indeed, he is finally saved from parricide only by Robespierre's suicide.

Tracing the process of developing the action, it will be found that act one passes in the forest of Montmorency, where in a somewhat formal fashion the facts in the case are presented. Robespierre enters, and during his interview with Vaughn, the Englishman who bears proposals from Fox, there is given a fine insight into the character of the " Incorruptible." The scene ends with the arrest of Clarise and Marie. The first scene of act two, located in the courtyard of the Prison Port Libre, is thrilling in its suggested horror, but it contributes but little toward the growth of the action. Scene two, the fête of the Supreme Being, is a brilliant spectacle, but it does not advance the play, until the moment for Olivier's arrest comes, just before the fall of the curtain.

Act three, which occurs in Robespierre's lodgings in the house of Duplay, is by far the strongest of the five. The interview between father and son, on the one side yearning affection and on the other bitter hate, is finely dramatic. The manner in which Robespierre learns the truth regarding Olivier is subtly conceived, and the obstinacy of the boy, who, misinterpreting Robespierre's motives, refuses to tell in what prison his mother and sweetheart are confined, is a tremendously strong counter force. Scene one of the fourth act brings out the fact of the rescue of Clarise and her companion and the miscarriage of the plans regarding Olivier; and it also pictures the grief-stricken father and mother, watching the passing by of the tumbrils, bearing the condemned to the guillotine, the two in dreadful fear lest their son be among those riding in the death-carts. The episode is wholly theatrical and not especially effective. Equally artificial and equally unsatisfactory is the second scene of the same act, representing Robespierre visited by the shades of his victims, a Shakespearian conception without the Shakespearian sincerity. The two scenes of the last acts, both dealing with the riotous convention that overthrew Robespierre, are remarkable scenic achievements, though the final moment is weakened by an anticlimax.

Henry Irving as Robespierre was to be credited with the making of an intensely interesting character, one finely imagined, closely analysed, and then conveyed to the audience with sure intellectual grasp. The Irving mannerisms and grotesques were less pronounced and less offensive in "Robespierre" than in many other of his impersonations. In nothing that this actor does, however, are they entirely absent. Mr. Irving's character exposition in the first act was clear and acute, and the trying moments of the third act were carried through with dignity, power, and sincerity. The emotion aroused by the passing of the tumbrils in the fourth act was clouded at times, though the effect in the main was vivid and impressive. The beginning of the "ghost" scene was creepy, but the conclusion was marred by an excessive display of the Irving peculiarities of voice and bodily pose. The concluding scene in the convention was well conceived, and was worked up to the moment of suicide with sustained climactic power. The suicide itself, however, was a distinct drop.

Yet, allowing all excellent in his impersonation, it was nevertheless true that Mr. Irving won his greatest triumph in "Robespierre" as a stage-manager. Some were not greatly impressed with the quality of Sardou's play considered as a work of dramatic art, and others cavilled at certain phases in Mr. Irving's presentation of the leading part, but no one could justly deny the thoroughness and the effectiveness of Mr. Irving's stage-management. There is nothing harder to handle on the stage than a crowd. One can drill with comparatively little trouble a number of men and women to shout together and to wave their arms together; but when one begins to strive for independent action, and to teach each man and woman in a crowd to shout without regard for what his companions are doing, and to wave his arms as if he were the only person anywhere in sight, there is difficulty, and plenty of it, right away. There is naturally in a stage crowd neither spontaneity nor a sense of personal responsibility; and it was in getting his masses to simulate spontaneity and to assume personal responsibility that Mr. Irving was most successful.

As a case in point there was the convention in " Robespierre," a scene of considerable length, in which the interest depended as much upon the supernumeraries as upon the actors.

The mob must have not only spontaneity and naturalness, but it must also display variety in its emotions and methods of expression. Mr. Irving's setting of the stage was of itself unique. On the rising of the curtain one found himself looking into an amphitheatre. The centre of the stage was clear. On the left, as the spectators saw it, was the tribunal, from which the convention was addressed, and above that the president's desk. Extending from the right of the stage in a curve around the rear were the tiers of seats, occupied by the excited members of the convention. The gathering filled the eye completely, and by a seeming overflow into galleries partially in sight, the effect of still greater numbers was secured. The realism of the turbulent assemblage was superb. Here was a mob that really acted, and that was vitally concerned in the action. How perfect the roars and the mutterings, the deafening applause and the apprehensive silence, the whisperings, the gesticulations, the cries of fanatical joy when the speakers uttered the magic words, " Liberty, equality, fraternity ! "

In preparing the colourful picture of prison

life, Mr. Irving was confronted with a different problem.   He had not only to give his crowd action and movement, but he had also to touch it with pathos, and to add, if possible, a sense of impending tragedy.   In the latter matter Mr. Irving was not successful.   He did, however, succeed in creating a distinct feeling of pathos.   It was remarkable how painstakingly and how intelligently the individualities of the different prisoners were brought out.   This careful discrimination made the episode of the reading of the names of the condemned one of unusual variety in the emotions portrayed and suggested.   As a background, contrasting with the gloomy terror and horrible brutality of the action, was ever in evidence the pride and the dignity, even the vivacity and the gaiety of the French aristocrat.   Inspiring courage in facing death, surpassing generosity, and noble self-sacrifice were shown, and the contrasting notes of cowardly fear and blank despair were by no means forgotten.

Except for the quality of its stage-management, " Robespierre " would not have attracted any great attention.   It won its success, not because it was an interesting or even an entertaining play, but because it was a remarkable spectacle. Its dramatic value was of the slightest, and what it had depended entirely on the exposition of the character of Robespierre. In that part, Mr. Irving once more showed his surpassing ability as a character actor. The part, however, did not reach the heart; it was too superficial. Sardou used Robespierre as an instrument by means of which to play upon his audiences' susceptibilities. He was ever calculating, this Frenchman, ever balancing this situation against that situation, throwing in a bit of suspense here, — as a mason might slap down an extra daub of mortar before placing a brick in position, — and increasing the stress of the emotion there. Always he had the tail of his eye fixed on those who were seated in the darkened auditorium beyond the footlights, and a mighty poor opinion he had of them, it would occasionally appear, judging by the quality of some of the matter he presented for their delectation and approval.

CHAPTER XII.

MRS. FISKE

BY reason of her unique personality, her high artistic ideal, her sturdy independence, her worthy accomplishments, and, crowning all, her evident intelligence, Mrs. Fiske occupies a position in the American theatre both prominent and isolated. She stands aloof from any class, coterie, or clique. She is herself, doing her work in her own way, imitating no one, and borrowing neither method nor idea. She is the single player on the American stage that absolutely refuses to be classified. Neither comedian nor tragedian, neither emotionalist nor romanticist, she is distinctly individual; and being intelligent as well as individual, she presents to the discriminating critic adequate and conclusive reasons why she should be judged by herself. Rigidly limited in her means of expression, utilising at all times and in all characters a hard, staccato, and even monotonous histrionic style, speaking with a voice that is unmusical and incapable of varied colouring, plain of face, small of stature, of unimpressive stage presence, handicapped right and left, so it would seem, by these physical disabilities, Mrs. Fiske, nevertheless, is to be counted one of the most versatile, one of the most satisfactory, and assuredly, one of the most original and unconventional actors in the United States.

Nor is there any mystery why this should be so. Mrs. Fiske's stage career has been nothing short of extraordinary in its versatility. Beginning as a child actress, and playing all sorts of characters, from Shakespearian boys to melodramatic old women, she first starred as the rival of Lotta and Maggie Mitchell in soubrette or "protean" parts. Years of hard work have given Mrs. Fiske her present position. She is not weird nor strange nor incomprehensible. She did not flash before one as a phenomenon, fascinating because unknown, alluring because unaccountable, interesting because unexpected. She is there to be studied and to be understood; and the more she is

LOTTA
From an old engraving

studied, and the better she is understood, the more potent becomes her spell, and the more certain her attractiveness. Mrs. Fiske is not a fleeting impression, she is not exotic, she is not morbid, she is not sensational. Her art is solid fact; her reputation has been a steady growth; her accomplishments are the definite results of definite purpose. In short, Mrs. Fiske not only has the artistic temperament, but she has as well the technical equipment to make her temperament do the work that she wants it to do.

Actors depend on various factors for their effects. Some rely almost entirely on personality, some on physical beauty, others on winsome ways or dashing vigour, or drooping sentiment, or flamboyant advertising. All these things are undignified, trivial, without permanence or stability. Mrs. Fiske depends on none of them. She goes straight to the source of all vital action and all enduring achievement — the infinite power of mind. Mentally she comprehends, at least to a perceptible and measurable degree, the full scope of the drama, and the fact that she does comprehend so much makes possible the conviction, the positive appeal, the truth, and the suggestive power manifested in her acting. It is a fact that her results are usually inferior in scope and in force to the broad sweep of her conception, but even with this disability and limitation she is still remarkably effective, undeniably inspiring, and inherently ennobling. Thinking always for herself, labouring continually to convey a mental impression with as little as possible of the intervening physical mediumship to distract one's attention, Mrs. Fiske makes her most insistent attack, not on the eye nor on the ear, but on the understanding. She spurs the thought, for she strives to impress the intelligence.

Mrs. Fiske has been termed a " realistic " actress. Many of those who have thus expressed themselves regarding her acting have simply meant that she uses very few gestures and very little bodily action to indicate emotion and to elaborate character. Recognising, as one must, if he has gathered from her acting anything more than an external impression, that she always strikes directly at the intelligence, one can understand why she is realistic in the sense indicated above. Her entire purpose being to focus the thought of her audience on the character that she is interpreting, and on the emotion that she is presenting, she has no use nor any need for unnecessary externals. In fact, any merely ornamental action would be worse than useless to her, for the moment that the attention was drawn from her mental conception to the physical means wherewith the mental conception was being expressed, that moment Mrs. Fiske would lose her complete sway of the individual consciousness. Her spell would be broken, and she would become no longer strictly an interpretative agent, but she would appear in the lesser light of a mechanical fact and figure. Fully to appreciate the quality of her work, one must keep his thought firmly fixed on the mental states that she is illustrating.

That Mrs. Fiske moves one only so long as she interests one intellectually, I have proved by seeing her several times in the same impersonation. Experiencing her for the first time in a new part, she has never failed to hold me entirely and to impress me deeply. She has done this regardless of the quality of the play in which she has appeared. Watching her several times in the same part, however, I have felt this interest, or rather this absorption, in her acting vanish; and then there has been revealed to me, what I had not in the first instance noticed — the wonderful mechanics of her work. All that had before appeared so natural, so spontaneous, so directly expressive of the instantaneous impression, and so thoroughly and so artistically realistic, was found to be as fixed, as determined, and as certain as the perfect engine, smooth-running and positive in its action, though highly intricate and complicated in its workings. Yet, thus becoming conscious of the externals of Mrs. Fiske's art meant a great sacrifice of illusion. While these externals interest and impress one, they do not convince. In attending to them, the thought is wrongly focussed — on the expression of the object — instead of on the object expressed.

Mrs. Fiske's ability to make an inferior play interesting was illustrated during the season of 1901–02 by her work in " The Unwelcome Mrs. Hatch," a four-act comedy of which Mrs. Burton Harrison was the author. The play dealt with social life in modern New York, but was chiefly notable from the fact that it afforded Mrs. Fiske exceptional opportunities for the display of the quality of suppressed and deep-seated emotional acting of which she is a particular and a peculiarly effective exponent. Considered apart from its workmanship, Mrs. Harrison's play was bountiful in its dramatic material, keen in its native interest, showing situations that suggested emotional intensity, strong in its leading characters, and direct and lucid in its dialogue. Unfortunately, its feeble and uncertain construction clouded and diminished all its good points. It lacked the finishing and pointed touches that a dramatist in command of the technique of his craft would have given it as a matter of course. It was evident that the knack of telling a story so that it should convince eye and ear and imagination at one and the same time — the knack that makes the dramatist somewhat different from the novelist — had not found its way into Mrs. Harrison's pen. Only the originality of the character that Mrs. Fiske portrayed, and the actress's fine grasp of its definite psychology, together with her vivid and realistic presentation of its moods and counter-moods, atoned for the naïveness with which the play itself was built.

The unwelcome Mrs. Hatch, so one learned in the play, was in reality Mrs. Marion Lorimer, divorced wife of Richard Lorimer, and mother of Gladys Lorimer, who was on the point of being married. Years before, the Lorimers' home life had been wrecked by the advent of a second woman. In a despairing moment, over the loss of her husband's affection, Mrs. Lorimer had written a compromising letter and left her home. The letter was sufficient to procure Lorimer his divorce and enable him to marry the woman who was the cause of his domestic difficulties. Gladys grew up, believing her own mother to be dead. The divorced Mrs. Lorimer, or Mrs. Hatch, as she called herself, left New York and remained away until a notice of her daughter's approaching marriage made the longing of her mother's love too strong to be resisted; and to appease that longing, she reëntered the zone of her suffering. The sight of her daughter in the park made the desire to be near her, to touch her, to help array her in her wedding finery, all the greater. By a subterfuge, the

MRS. FISKE

Lorimer in " The Unwelcome Mrs. Hatch "

mother stole into her former husband's home, tasted joy unspeakable in a precious interview with the girl, and endured bitter ignominy and shame in the meeting with Lorimer and his wife that followed.

The thread of her endurance snapped with this last strain, and the body succumbed, though the spirit continued strong to the end. The last scene depicted the passing away of the unfortunate woman, victim of an ironical fate, at the very moment when the dawn of happiness was appearing. I confess that Mrs. Hatch's death struck me as wilful rather than inevitable. Like many others, I prefer a happy ending, when a happy ending is as logical and as truthful as a sorrowful one. There is no especial art-virtue in death, unless death be represented as the punishment for unrepented or unatoned-for evil. Mrs. Hatch's fault had been that of weakness, and she had more than atoned for it by her suffering and unhappiness. To kill her for it, savoured of wanton murder. It seemed an arbitrary harassing of an audience's sensibilities to continue the poor woman's hard luck right up to final tragedy of six feet of sod, when, with a son and a daughter and an honest man all ready and anxious to love her and care for her, there was every chance of her living to a green old age with a fair degree of enjoyment.

Mrs. Fiske's Mrs. Hatch was a satisfying study of character from start to finish, analytically noteworthy, emotionally intense, and continually genuine, with a grasp of effect that reached, beyond the copying of life, straight into the higher art realm of establishing the illusion of life. Art is not photographic. A mere reproduction, however perfect in detail, has no value, unless it be enforced with a clear idea of reality in the thought of the one making the reproduction. Art does not deal with dry and barren facts, but with living, pulsating effects. Mrs. Fiske's eminence is not due to the method that she employs in her acting. It may be a very bad method — for somebody else. Her eminence is due to the effects that she produces, and these are often remarkable. She gets beneath the skin. She sights beyond the material manifestation. She gives glimpses of the true image and likeness that is within.

CHAPTER XIII.

HERE are two honours open to the woman who is seeking the "bubble reputation" in the theatre, the attaining of which marks her supreme artistic achievement and gives her ready rank among the immortals. One of these fame-crowned eminences is the passionate Juliet, ill-starred daughter of the Capulets; the other is the brilliant Rosalind, laughing-eyed and lovable-natured habitant of the Forest of Arden. Those there have been who have successfully scaled both these heights of character impersonation, and emblazoned their names thereupon in enduring letters. A few, also, there have been, who, denied the sweet triumphs of embodying with eternal idealism the two most beautiful and most lovely of the Shakespearian conceptions, have, nevertheless, conquered fame in the more heroic lines of endeavour, represented by Lady Macbeth and Queen Katharine. Preëminent — indeed, practically alone — in the latter group stand the majestic Siddons and the strong and mighty Cushman.

During the season of 1901–02, it was the happy lot and deserved fortune of Miss Henrietta Crosman to add her name to the long line of accomplished players, whom the weeding process of time has left as the best of all the many Rosalinds — a roll of beauty, of talent, and of potent charm that is headed by the dashing "Peg" Woffington, whose career in this part, inaugurated so gloriously in 1742, ended so tragically in 1757; a list that includes the tragedy-weighted and the foolishly prudish Mrs. Siddons, wearing, instead of the inconspicuous doublet and hose, a nondescript and ridiculous costume, designed to conceal as much as possible of her ample figure, but serving to accentuate all the more her mental immodesty; that includes also the jolly and rollicking, and not over-virtuous, Dora Jordan, who liked nothing better than to display her fine shape for the benefit of the town; the lithe and graceful Ellen Tree, the first of the notable English actresses to

ADELAIDE NEILSON

appear as Rosalind in the United States; the masculine Charlotte Cushman, altogether too ponderous and heavy to be acceptable as the merry, masquerading maiden; the beautiful and gentle Helen Faucit, sweetest and womanliest Rosalind of her time; the fascinating Mrs. Mowatt, and the alluring Adelaide Neilson; and last of all, until the sparkling and accomplished Crosman added her name to the number, the honoured four, rightly declared the best Rosalinds of the modern stage — the lovely and winsome Julia Marlowe, the dashing and imperious Ada Rehan, the dainty and vivacious Helena Modjeska, the statuesque and serenely beautiful Mary Anderson.

There are two Rosalinds common to the stage, — one a hearty and healthy girl, abounding in jovial spirits and thorough good fellowship; the other a more self-conscious and delicately feminine creature, winsome and wooing, dainty and refined. I acknowledge a preference for the first conception, which, however, has not been the popular one since Modjeska gained such wide-spread approval for her essentially feminine impersonation. Although not a large woman physically, Miss Crosman did succeed in bringing out the frank and wholesome robustness of Rosalind's nature, and this achievement gave her Rosalind a strength, an inspiration, a vivacity, and a spontaneity most enjoyable.

Appearing in " As You Like It " for the first time, and playing Rosalind for the first season, signs of youthfulness and inexperience there undoubtedly were in Miss Crosman's work; but even with those in view, it was immediately and vigorously manifested that she was in no need of an apologist. Her Rosalind was a definite characterisation. It is to be expected that, with increased confidence and augmented facility, with fuller understanding and added elaboration, she will develop a Rosalind more complete in detail, more suggestive in mood and motive, and more comprehensive in womanliness. It would indeed be a reflection on her art and a blot on her reputation, if her further acquaintance with this complex and fascinating Shakespearian creation did not result in additional authority and incisiveness. Nevertheless, always holding in thought the ideal of perfection as a vigorous incentive to harder work and deeper thought, there is every reason why the warmest commendation should be given the present achievement.

Miss Crosman's personal attractiveness is exceedingly great. It added much to the effectiveness of her Mistress Nell, and it was equally zealous in advancing the interests of her Rosalind. Fortunate the player that never has to argue an audience into accepting him! In fact, Miss Crosman at once goes, on the instant of her appearance, a step beyond the notion of mere acceptance; she makes an audience resolute in its intention to like her and to like her very much. She fascinates at first sight, and naturally, after that favourable and receptive condition has been established, she finds the burden of interesting and con- vincing comparatively easy. Her Rosalind carried so much of this winning personality, especially in the captivating Forest of Arden scenes, that it really was difficult sufficiently to separate the charm of the actress from the character she was portraying to be able to de- clare positively what manner of woman she was mentally declaring Rosalind to be.

Of course, such an admission as that means only one thing — it is the sincerest praise that can be given to a player's art; it betokens the actor thoroughly identified with his part. Acting, so natural that it is difficult to determine precisely in what particular it is acting, is assuredly the best acting that there can be. Miss Crosman's Rosalind certainly did have much of this art so fine in quality that it really seemed to be artlessness. Her spontaneity, vivacity, maidenliness, and half bashful boldness in the delicious forest talks with Orlando were felt as realities, and feeling them as realities, enjoying them to the limit and bent on drawing from them every drop of the honeyed fragrance, one was not troubling himself much about deducing Rosalind's possible mental state. There is a vital difference between feeling that a thing is so, and arguing one's self into believing that a thing is so because there is external evidence to prove the contention. With Miss Crosman's Rosalind the reality appeared as a fact to be accepted without argument. One was convinced, and that was the end of the matter.

Having voiced so much praise, it may be well to go back a trifle, lest this Rosalind be so overweighted with virtues that her real merits are either forgotten or ignored. As between over-praise and under-valuation, better choose the latter evil; it at least asserts a demand for further effort, and it leaves a chance for bettered impression. I am not willing to consider Miss Crosman's work in any way finished. She has modelled her statue in noble and striking outline, but she has not chiselled it in imperishable marble. Her Rosalind is not yet from beginning to end one unmistakable woman. The very essential quality of clearness — of knowing exactly what she wants to say, and then saying it in plain, straightforward fashion — is not so much in evidence as it should be. There remain moments when one feels that her conception wavers and is not quite at ease.

Practically every actress that has ever tried to act Rosalind has succeeded in giving a fairly satisfactory view of Rosalind's superficial qualities — her merry humour, her wit, her intense delight in a jest, her very feminine bantering and raillery, her romantic love. But these, though important factors, are, after all, only attributes — they are not the real Rosalind. Back of them is the rich womanliness that could instantly attract and permanently hold a youth of Orlando's lofty ideality, the resoluteness of purpose and the strength of character that would never permit her fine spirit to be dampened by the incoming of adversity, and the moral courage that could give her the ascendancy over chilling circumstance in spite of the handicap of her woman's body, the authority and poise that enabled her to meet a man as a man, and, meeting him, more than hold her own without the need of refuge in his chivalry.   The phrase, the weaker vessel, was not applicable to Rosalind.   Always decorated and embellished with rare humour and girlish fantasy, and often almost concealed by the more obvious delights of witchery of face, form, and personality, these solid characteristics, nevertheless, constitute the real Rosalind.   One felt them, too, in Miss Crosman's delineation, but he did not feel quite sure that the actress herself recognised them for their full value.   In so far as she held them necessary to the expression of her conception, just so far her acting partook of the highest quality of character realisation.

Having, by her assumption of Rosalind, fully

MAXINE ELLIOTT

As Portia in " The Merchant of Venice."

proved her right to rank as a talented player of Shakespearian comedy, Miss Crosman finds open to her a noble and important field of histrionic endeavour. It is an astonishing and lamentable fact that, during the season of 1901–02, her production of " As You Like It " was the only Shakespearian enterprise to attract wide-spread attention in the United States. Shakespeare was played to some extent by the local stock companies and on the minor circuits — notably by Modjeska, who acted in " King John "; but Miss Crosman's Rosalind was the only Shakespearian character to be seen in the leading theatres. This is a suggestive commentary on the short-sightedness of the commercial manager, for it is not true that the public will not patronise Shakespeare when it is adequately given. The experience of Miss Crosman as Rosalind, of Mr. Mansfield as Henry V., of Mr. Sothern as Hamlet (though he made the essay at his own expense and against the advice of his manager, Daniel Frohman, who refused to share the financial responsibility), of Mr. Goodwin and Miss Elliott as Shylock and Portia, of Miss Adams as Juliet — though it may be justly argued that these last two enterprises had too much of the circus about them to be a fair test of anything except the personal popularity of the players — make it reasonably manifest that there is a real demand for Shakespeare. This does not mean, naturally, that Shakespeare and nothing else is wanted. There is a demand for every good thing from farce to tragedy, and I thoroughly believe that at the present time first place in our theatre belongs rightfully to the modern drama and especially to the worthy American play; but this does not mean that there is no solid success awaiting the actor who helps to maintain the Shakespearian drama in the honourable position that it should have on the English-speaking stage.

Now that Julia Marlowe has practically deserted the higher class of drama, it would appear that an especially important and noble work has fallen upon Miss Crosman. The mental and physical requirements to essay successfully the Shakespearian women are by no means common, and Miss Crosman has her fair share of them, at least in so far as comedy is concerned. Judging by so much of her art as she has made manifest up to the present moment, it would be absurd for her to attempt the broader and more vigorous impersonations. She is not fitted to play Queen Katharine, and probably not Lady Macbeth, though personal charm has occasionally done wonders with that character. Juliet would also seem to be out of Miss Crosman's line, as would Katharina in " The Taming of the Shrew," which Ada Rehan has made so firmly her own that the player trying the part at the present moment would have much prejudice to overcome. Desdemona, Ophelia, and Portia, Miss Crosman is debarred from, unless she is willing to share her stellar honours, though that she would make interesting all three parts, I am quite confident. As Rosalind and Viola, and possibly as Beatrice and Imogen, Miss Crosman has ample scope for labour both varied and valuable.

CHAPTER XIV.

THESE volumes have been written from the fundamental proposition that the stage is by its very nature an accurate and direct reflection of the thought of the people. The art-instinct of the English-speaking nations has always expressed itself with greatest freedom and with noblest results in literature, rather than in painting, sculpture, or music; and the early glories of the English drama were due to the fact that practically the entire literary thought of that period was fixed on the theatre. Poets and story-tellers, satirists, and even historians, looked upon the drama as a natural means of expression and a necessary means of publicity. Through the medium of the play, their thoughts and theories were brought directly to the notice of the cultured and discriminating public.

After a time, however, the educated public

became too large and too diversified in its tastes for the theatre alone to satisfy. The printing-press was loudly calling for copy, and printed literature came into existence to meet the demand for a vehicle of thought-expression less limited in its circulation than the acted play. Feeling the fascination that is ever found in some new thing, the advent of the novel and the newspaper turned many, who under the old conditions would have been makers of drama, into the unexplored channels of printed fact and fiction. The most intelligent of the public, quickly seizing, as is its wont, upon the fresh and the original, discovered, in the direct appeal to the imagination made by the novel, a delight that it had never experienced from the formal theatricalism of the old time tragedy. Revelling in the historical colouring and the vivid characterisation of Sir Walter Scott, in his romance and mysticism, they forgot that such a thing as the theatre existed. Thus deprived of the patronage of both writer and critical public, theatrical taste, and with it stage literature, declined to almost nothing, the play lost its standing as an ennobling pleasure, and the drama became the

Ishmaelite among the arts. The edict of the Puritan against the stage of the Charleses was revived, and prejudice and ignorance outside the theatre vied with prejudice and ignorance inside the theatre to debase and eternally damn an institution that by right and heritage should be both profitable and entertaining. Dishonoured in the house of its friends, and degraded in the councils of its enemies, the loftiest purpose of a theatre which had fostered the genius of a Shakespeare, a Jonson, a Congreve, a Goldsmith, and a Sheridan, was to "give the public what it wanted."

During the century of its literary non-existence, the sole glory of the English theatre was in its players, a gifted group of men and women, who, bred and nurtured on the strong meat of the Shakespearian drama, sacrificed much to keep alive the traditions of good acting. For two and a half centuries, Shakespeare was the single steady and enduring influence in the English theatre, the balance-wheel, the standard, and the ideal. While Shakespeare made actors, he did not, however, make dramatists. The majesty of his genius forbade even feeble imitation. When he ended his work, it was finished for all time.　The path which he had blazed through the virgin forest marked the only way to the apex of the mountain that he had chosen to climb; and in this path might walk disciples and followers, but no rivals.

Shakespeare, great as he was, did not cover the whole range of the drama; and when, as a feeble growth after many years of barrenness, a new English drama began to appear, the theatre-going public, then made up almost entirely of the "plain people," whose emotions were strong and sincere and easily moved, but whose thought lacked reliable taste and training, became blindly intoxicated with the strange dramatic novelty that gave them a glimpse of things that they knew about, things that they themselves had felt and could therefore comprehend at first hand.　Forsaking, after Robertson became the vogue, the Shakespearian balance-wheel that had been their surety for generations, they plunged madly into wild and indiscriminate excesses.　Everything that had once claimed their devoted attention was forthwith completely neglected, Shakespeare and the Shakespearian actor with the rest; and in the unprincipled mêlée that followed the formula of "giving the public what it wanted" got in its deadliest work.

However, the more unseemly the excess, the quicker the reaction. There is evidence to show that the demand for a higher class of drama than that which has occupied nearly the whole of the theatre-going public for thirty years past is already active. It is a fact also that printed fiction is now suffering from the same ungoverned taste that has worked so disastrously in the theatre. One compliments neither the novelist nor the dramatist when he declares that there are about the same number of great novelists to-day as there are great dramatists, and that the average novel of the present moment is worth just about as much as the average play, which too often is dramatised from it. The same tendency of materialism to twist the rope wherewith to hang itself is likewise seen in the newspaper, which has sacrificed the birthright of true journalism for a mess of pottage represented in the collection and distribution of tea-table gossip and drawing-room scandal. The world advances in sections, so it would seem; and judging by the signs of the times, the theatrical section is even now stepping forward. What is to-day chiefly hiding and hindering the real condition in public taste, is the commercial manager, who, unable himself to lead the way, and not content to walk meekly and modestly in the rear, insists on loading down the chariot of progress with his own dead weight and with the further incumbrance of his precious money bags.

What will be the future of the theatre? Why try to limit the range of possibilities by any statement of probabilities? One thing only is certain — as the thought of the people broadens and expands and reaches upward, so the theatre will gain in dignity, in worthiness, and in elevation. There is even now a mighty influence working in the minds of men, the full effect of which no mortal can at this moment determine. Already it has been deeply felt in the religious world, renovating wornout creeds and upsetting formal theological doctrines. Its next attack will be on the world of art, and there, too, false theories and tarnished dogmas will be pulled down and cast forth. True religion and true art are but two different phases of one and the same thing, and they both should express man's highest ideal of eternal truth. This regenerating influence, the presence of which is being manifested so generally among thinking men and women, voices the power of good in opposition to the claims of rebellious evil. Its uplifting message is the immortality of optimism ; its sturdy declaration is for ideality in the place of the crass and degrading realism of material sense ; its insistent demand is for truth. This is the influence which will dictate the new drama and which will mould the new theatre.

THE END.